deAd liNeS

robert majzels

deAd liNeS

ROBERT MAJZELS

Zat-So Productions

flies in the face of reason

published by Zat-So Productions,
Montréal, Québec
First edition 2023
All rights reserved
zatso.productions@gmail.com

ISBN: 978-0-9867595-6-7 (softcover b/w)

The author thanks Erín Moure for her encouragement and keen editorial eye.
The characters depicted in this work are all recycled in accordance with the author's commitment to reducing the production of single-use characters.

Cover image by Robert Majzels
Cat's Eye Nebula images by J.P. Harrington and K.J. Borkowski (University of Maryland) and NASA/ESA, alterations by Robert Majzels
Excerpts from Gerrard Winstanley, *The True Levellers Standard Advanced (1649)*, University of Oregon, 2002
Citation on p. 106 is from L.H. Berens, *The Digger Movement in the Days of the Commonwealth*, 2006, Project Gutenberg.

The author acknowledges the financial assistance of the Canada Council for the Arts

Canada Council   Conseil des arts
for the Arts   du Canada

Zat-So Productions
flies in the face of reason

Why should the novelist believe he is obligated to explain the behavior of his characters, and to supply them with reasons, whereas life for its part never explains anything and leaves in its creatures so many indeterminate, obscure, indiscernible zones that defy any attempt at clarification?

Gilles Deleuze
"Bartleby; or The Formula"
trans. D. W. Smith and M. A. Greco

Mais, en vérité, il n'y a pas de prose.

Stéphane Mallarmé
interviewed by Jules Huret in *l'Écho de Paris, 1891*

People say I'm difficult and I have no hits. And they say that like it's a bad thing.

Tom Waits
speech at the *Rock and Roll Hall of Fame*

modestement

under a red radioactive sky the air thick with smoke from the fires to the south bObby 2shOes lay low. in a stand of withered aspens measuring the distance across the open stretch to the leVeLLeRs' vegetable patch good news no fence around the garden leVeLLeRs did not believe. in fences which mattered little because nothing worth eating lay on the small mound where they usually left carrots for the few remaining deer and demented raccoons meanwhile and it was a truly mean. while. that boy we called 2shOes because he had none which made their absence a constant preoccupation that boy cast a wary eye. on the rows of blighted potato plants you may be wondering where and when had Bobby 2shoes lost. his shoes. perhaps he'd never had any i don't recall even though i was that. boy

that deadline's come and gone
these dead lines all that remains
now we're deAdliNeRs
deAdliNeRs in the outlands

heat fire flood locusts plague

deAdliNeRs nurture our rage
deAdliNeRs live these final days
exacting the crumbs of revenge
on the bubbled few

bObby 2shOes crouch-running from the scrub and
withered aspens over dust and dirt to a dozen rows
of potato plants where he lay flat and motionless. for
a couple of long minutes that patch was one sad crop
of rhizomes even bObby 2shOes could tell and what
2shOes knew about vegetable gardening never mind
potatoes you could fit in a hand. trowel no make that
a seed sachet a snail's shell a common bean pod
between two hands praying and the fires to the south

that potato patch promised very little a dozen short rows of pale yellow leaves squatting. on the grey turf why the leVeLLers even bothered all that labour for such a meagre. reward as far as bObby 2shOes and the deAdliNeRs were concerned the leVeLLers had capitulated their passive acceptance of a cruel and criminal situation abandoning the war. against the buBBles to scratch out a less than subsistence livelihood in the barren ground and poisoned lakes huddling. around camp fires and singing ritualized folk songs to keep cold nights at bay

he lay flat between two rows. in the garden pausing to catch his breath hacking and spitting a gob of dark phlegm he'd brought no tools not even. a stick so he used his hands to scrabble at the dusty bed until he could pull the potato up from the ground grip the hard black knuckle tear it from the main. stem and slip it into the pocket of his ragged jeans

a thousand years ago a star
cast off its outer material envelope
and the cAt's eYe nebula was born
in violent interaction
a fast stellar wind driving
previously ejected material
the inner bubble hollowed out

here the image of my father in his lawn chair
eyes squeezed shut one arm bent
fingers resting tent-like on his forehead
and the pulse of Oświęcim inside his head

bObby 2shOes had bellied along a few inches begun to claw the ground for a second potato when he saw. the leVeLLer coming toward him between the rows she was tall elderly but unbent white haired grim faced a quick glance behind. revealed a teenager approaching a slight limp from the other end of the row this paragraph could be reshaped into a poem 2shOes wasn't really worried weren't the leVeLLers famous for their nonviolence still they had recently made angry noises about the deAdliNeRs their occasional raids sporadic pillaging and this time 2shOes propelled. by the hunger engine. had come in alone he pushed up to his knees preparing to talk or run that's when the woman coming toward him reached behind and produced. the rifle. she'd been carrying on her back her entire adult life three thousand light-years. from eARTh under the dying gaze of NGC 6543 the cAt's eYe nebula had been the fanatical focus. of dOctOr suZaNNe poNt-l'éVeQue's telescopic attention now in retirement and denied access. to the huBBle-weBB-liPPerhey's telescopic universe she turned her attention. to her own. death. and to the death. of her own planet the two appearing for the first time. in history at least from a scientific perspective very nearly concurrent

lent et triste

fugue grave sur le même sujet
lately and from time to time
the apocalypse winks at us
still and yet it's business as usual
another deadline's come and gone

close up before. she put on her pathomask he could
see. she was white deep tanned and wind wizened but
definitely white no surprise there weren't a lot of
white folks outside. the buBBles but most of the
LeVeLLers were white folks who'd made a bad
decision somewhere down the line some had
dropped out of the rat race then the buBBles walled
them out for good don't bolt. the woman said wagged
the barrel of the rifle at him we only want a bit of a
blab still she kept the rifle level waved him. in the
direction of the buildings more like shacks and sheds
grouped around a larger two-floor structure of
distressed wood variously coloured bricks and
corrugated tin

en zézayant

green grass bird song still water
a momentary stability
false temporary doomed
and the fires to the south

observation data
right ascension	$17^h\ 58^m\ 33.423^s$
declination	$+66°\ 37'\ 59.52"$
distance	3.3 ±0.9 kly (1.0 ± 0.3 kpc) kly
apparent magnitude	9.8B
apparent dimensions core	20"

allez modérément
we were the small-scale structures of our planet
we were knots and jets and filaments
suZaNNe poNt-l'éVeQue
when she was DOCTOR poNt-l'éVeQue
cosmic eschatologist
because science likes to place things
into their proper bins
she'd learned to classify and categorize to add
and subjectivize and juggle algorithms
planetary nebulae of pieMbert type 1 type 2 type 3
friends colleagues acquaintances string pencils
bills of divorce hands stems minor characters
holy things animal sacrifices coats scarves figs
bread and butter

avec conviction et une tristesse rigoureuse
tossed my ink and brush
wrote with bits of string and sticks
once we searched for patterns
among nebulous explosions in the night sky
now we focus on this final pinpoint
glimmer of light
but that could be the light of those fires to the south

walking toward the dwellings she pulls a homemade
short wooden pipe blows a warning three leVeLLers
hooking pathomasks on their ears step into the
clearing between. the field. and the shelters to
welcome the intruder or maybe not welcome maybe
more like surround anyway one tall male about the
same age as the woman on the business end. of the
rifle but bearded under his mask mostly bald except
for a couple random tufts of hair and white though
darkish and creased from field work but sturdy the
other two are younger women also sturdy one blond
hair in ponytails the other big black afro

you been stealing here before the woman with the rifle says bObby 2shOes shrugs boy's not worried not yet anyway although. the rifle that's something new something to think about where he wonders did they get it only the buBBle patrols come strapped the few guns the deAdliNeRs enjoy have come by stealing or by ambushing the armed goons maybe you're hungry the man says looking him over the yellow ponytail scoffs maybe teach him how to grow potatoes she says give a man a fish and all that thought. you. leVeLLers were all no violence bObby 2shOes says. slowly nodding at the long gun maybe we got tired of deAdliNeRs stealing our grub the woman toting says bObby 2shOes sweeps a hand back in the direction of the potatoes you don't own this patch of dirt he says maybe not the beard says but we work it the cAucAsiAn cHalK ciRcLe and all that

the central bright part of NGC6543 consists of the
inner ellipse an elongated buBBle filled with hot gas
and nested in a pair of larger spherical buBBles
conjoined together along their waist the result is the
celestial phenomenon dubbed the cAt's eYe nebula

au pas camarade au pas
wrapped in the fold of repetition
ear to the barren ground listening
to hear myself speak silence
writing long gone lines
to the absent reader
and the fires to the south

what shall we do with him the rifle says and her rhetorical tone suggests she already has an idea the beard tilts his head from side. to. side maybe bObby figures maybe he's the soft one in the hard cop soft cop routine anyway the beard says maybe he bObby'd like to hang. a while share our food do some work no strings attached see how you like it bObby 2shOes lets the offer hang I'm not a deAdliNeR he says

strictly speaking that was not. a lie the deAdliNeRs are not. a card-carrying organization not remotely no unified leadership no coordination not even much. contact between packs numbering anything from two to two dozen organisms at the edge of life *comme une fleur fanée*

now we know the sun is dying
soon in cosmic time to be a burning nebula
the earth all dust and wind
now we know this
can we forget posterity
posterity is behind us we're sitting on our posterity
while we're at it shouldn't we forget
the absent reader
lay down the weapons of composition

brutal

dOctOr poNt-l'éVeQue's astronomical task
had been to produce the anamorphic image
                of the universe
                or some small part of it
through which one species on this distant planet
might know everything

calmement quatre-vingt cinq

now these *dead* lines
a *silk thread* pulls at
a line of *thought* by the *water's edge*
four dead lines of verse

the leVeLLers' common house was a more elaborate
and solid structure than the surrounding individual.
shelters and testimony to the leVeLLers' skills
constructed of deeply distressed. wood and tin it
contained a kitchen and meeting room with an
assortment of pews benches and chairs two grey-
ponytailed women were busy cutting pale carrots and
marble. sized potatoes on a long counter by a fire pit
in which he could see twigs and bits of broken
furniture one of the women turned and smiled at the
intruder they both paused to don masks. and got
back to work

d'une manière très particulière
there were self-shocking winds and mass fallback
a stellar wind blowing
a stellar wind blowing hard
a wind that hollowed out the inner bubble
of the nebula and burst that bubble
at both ends
meanwhile the cat on suZaNNe's windowsill
paid close attention

one parsec or 31 trillion kilometres
19 trillion miles 3.26 light-years
the distance between herself and those around her
those we classify as friends and family anyway that
was how she felt

she measured those distances by an object's
trigonometric parallax

you can do this by taking two measurements six
months apart

some friends and family were so far away that their
parallactic and proper motions were below the
threshold of measurement

the beard spots bObby 2shOes gazing. at a bowl brimming with water on the counter beside the cooks we collect some rainwater in those big vats you saw on the way in the beard tells him he smiles and shrugs at 2shOes's look of incredulity rain being rare enough. in this world that some young children have never seen it when it falls it ain't drinkable there's a well the beard says it's far to travel but the ground water out there's not poisoned our water's clean he moves on no propane so twigs is what we've got for fire the composting toilet and cans are out back he stops in the entrance to let bObby 2shOes take it. all in we call this place liTTle hEAth he says and they call me bOOger that's right he offers a hand bOOger rOOney

en grelottant quatre-vingt cinq
this *reckless* line *offered up*
to the spirits of the dead
a horse that *looks like* a horse
but is not a horse

in her solitude occasionally she imagined an unseen companion another star perhaps a brown dwarf or a large gassy planet

bObby 2shOes hesitates to offer up his name as anyone would hesitate i mean well any deAdliNeR would but feeling awkward under the gaze of his hosts' expectations he finally surrenders. his name a dense cloudy silence fills the room until the rifle toting woman who'd greeted him outside blinks does a quick hop and skip in lieu of a curtsy and offers her name which turns out to be beTTy as for the others in the room they keep their names to themselves here the reader if there were one would deduce this verse is about naming what do we reveal. when we reveal our name what part or parts of our self or selves do we exclude what do we destroy when we name any one or thing meanwhile while we the author and absent reader grapple. with these questions bObby 2shOes's eyes the vegetables on the kitchen counter

the great majority of her fellow astronomers plied their trade searching for the origins of stars and planetary systems yearning for a glimpse of the beginning of time and space she on the other hand. turned her gaze toward the end the death of stars of time and space and light

dOctOr suZaNNe poNt-l'éVeQue studied the shapes of planetary nebulae but what. does the shape of anything tell us about the mystery of the thing itself when we look at the image of a nebula we are deceived by the projection effects which alter our perception a circle she said is simply a non-eccentric ellipse

poème en forme de quatre-vingt cinq noix de coco
we were all night working
for the *department* of lines
some lines *lacked sincerity*
all were *incomplete*

you must be hungry the smaller of the two women in
the kitchen says she's wearing a pair of improvised
glasses two non-matching lenses glued. together in
square wooden frames which along with her batik
mask completely obscures her face why don't you sit.
and have a bite they treat him nicely sit him down at
a table in the dining area with a plate of grey-tinged
greens and a cup of a strange berry juice bOOger
rOOney and the unnamed woman armed with an
afro sit down a few feet away to watch. him eat while
the rifle and beTTy on the end of it disappear

quatre-vingt cinq tout à fait à l'heure
wait for a line of verse
meanwhile *practise whistling* old bits
writing water on stone
all the old lines *vanish*

八五 死了

because the number *four* is *death*
four dead lines of verse
silk thread silk line *torn*
spirits of the dead

we've had some success with kale
the small asymmetrically bespectacled woman says

                                        à la longue

she measured stars
their mass size composition lifespan
their distance from her sun
stars formed in the more distant past
stars formed in the more recent past
all those stars were dying
many are already dead

her attention drifts on a stellar wind
blows her outward from a pair of companion stars
not unlike the interaction
the push and pull of a progenitor star
and her companion
cat's eyes
cosmic gaze

if you lay a hand
on her again you
will drown in a
river of pain and
hyenas will feast
on your flesh and
broken bones

kale is a sturdy plant less affected by ground pollutants and requiring less water the bespectacled woman offers this information freely a gift a useful tip as though bObby 2shOes could use it he could not bObby 2shOes is not. agriculturally inclined he wouldn't be able to distinguish the difference between a kale and a carrot top still the food. is okay much better than the scraps he's used to he can make out some unfamiliar spice in it maybe. salt

quantum entanglement two particles can be a large distance apart and still be part of a single system in which they exist neither in one state or the other but in a superposition of both

bell's paradox arises because quantum mechanics depends on probabilities so that particles have an indeterminate existence until they are observed

what puzzled her. was our inability to detect close companions did the cAt's eYe for example have a close companion was the invisibility of close companions caused by their being disrupted. or merged with the progenitor star or was the shape of bipolar nebulae simply the result of dust. surrounding the progenitor star and deflecting the star's outgoing winds in which case there is no companion

merely a dying star blowing wind and dust
out into dark empty space

the sun it turns out is surrounded by a magnetic field but perhaps more importantly in less than five billion years. from now our sun will burst turning all its surrounding planets into dust at which time all that remains will be a planetary nebula

in construction what is called site work includes the scope of work related to the exterior of a project **surveying grading excavation site utilities paving concrete work and landscaping** are all examples that can be included in site work projects

air à faire fuir

when he heard his name in someone's throat
he did not recognize himself
he was eight years old early morning on his knees
on the dusty road
watching ants toing and froing from their domed
home in the sand
that miniature world was all the world they knew
and he too was small and alone in the world
and in the smoke from the fires to the south

when he's done gorging beTTy reappears without
her rifle and it's time for a tour of the encampment
with her and bOOger the leVeLLers' camp they call
liTTle hEAth is barely an oasis in the surrounding.
desolation rolling dusty hills interrupted here. and
there. by thickets of pale sparsely leafed trees
meanwhile bObby 2shOes can see westward in the
distance the white capped stony mountain range that
separates them from the buBBle and the ocean
beyond

pieds nus

the absence of shoes becomes a constant
preoccupation

long minutes lie flat and motionless
huddled around dying embers
scrabbling at the dusty bed

this war we wage against the bubble at our core
the bubble at my core hollowed out
the image of my father in a lawn chair
on my knees prepared to talk or run

the happy few in the buBBle do not call themselves buBBlers oh no they are the deMocRaTic grEEn beLtS (dgb) and the leading dictators do not call themselves dictators nor even leaders they are the cOMMuNiTy cOOrdiNaTing cOMMittEE (ccc) some years ago the ccc had requested well request was their word for do this or die anyway they'd requested dOctOr poNt-l'éVeQue shift the focus of her work from watching the explosive death of the cAt's eYe to the eLoN mUsKian search for nEw eArtH which is the name for a planet that does not exist. yet and which humans yearn to colonize once they've squeezed the last drop of life out of their own

so no wonder nEw eArtH is astronomy's principal area of research meanwhile. the deMocRaTic grEEn beLtS (dgb) have turned their backs on what's left i mean the millions of humans and animals and other life forms dying of heat flood fire radiation hunger outside the buBBles hence the order. went down to suZaNNe poNt-l'éVeQue to switch her focus however by the time that order reached her desk dOctOr poNt-l'éVeQue had dropped. out of the world and vanished from view

liTTle hEAth's attempts at farming include a few rows of pale green vegetables which bObby 2shOes can't name along with the potato patch. in which he was captured and several strips and mounds of dirt abandoned as failed experiments and yet even this meagre harvest is more. than he's seen in leVeLLer camps to the east the ground here he notes has been recently watered

this will be our orchard bOOger rOOney tells him pointing to three bare sticks enclosed in a circle of barbed. wire pear trees rOOney announces oh i know they don't look like much right now but we're working on it each of the young trees is enthroned. in a ring of moist woody scraps

the workshop is a tin-covered wood shack the tools within mostly hoes and shovels gardening implements also an ancient circular. saw powered by a mechanism that looks like a bicycle rOOney plays guide but bObby 2shOes senses that beTTy's in charge watching him gauging his reactions

en zigouillant comme un zigoto
when he pulled a memory out of his head it made a
sound like the sound when you pull your foot up out
of the mud

also he noticed that when he spoke
the words came out of his mouth
with a sound just like that sound

when you stand in the shallow end of the lake
your feet swallowed in slime
that sucking lip-smack when you pull your foot out
of your mouth

en tirant la langue
the recurring question of audience
imagined in a future time
when the sun is red and dying
this planet turned to dust
and horked into the celestial void

bOOger rOOney with a wide sweeping gesture asks what do you think bObby 2shOes. shrugs what's the point at least we're doing something beTTy says we're feeding ourselves without harming the planet we're building a community 2shOes nods where're you getting the water what are you deAdliNeRs doing beTTy says raiding buBBles blowing up powerlines shooting a low ranked military out directing traffic knifing a clerk on his way to work not to mention she says pointing at the hollow imprint of bObby 2shOes's body where he'd lain in the potato patch stealing. the food we work hard. to grow

i'm not a deAdliNeR bObby 2shOes says

en allant promener
after he learned to drive my father bought a secondhand plyMouth belVedere with a lousy radiator that constantly. overheated suNdAy afternoons the family piled in and went for a drive out to the west island to ogle the homes of the rich occasionally my father could be heard to curse them under his breath otherwise we were silent and staring

34

she'd read in jeAn-fRaNÇois lyOtArD's *l'inHuMaiN*
the suggestion that the ultimate goal for science was
to prepare not only for the death of the sun which
may be too far in the future for us to truly imagine
but also for the destruction of all living beings on
eARTh which it entails this struck her as a noble
pursuit a vocation she could wholeheartedly assume

take it easy man says bOOger rOOney and lays a light
hand on bObby's shoulder we're just showing you
around

but who were they the ones who had found a place in the buBBles they were the oil barons the auto makers politicians captains of industry commodity traders executives of mining and logging and pesticide and fertilizer companies emperors of tech buyers and sellers. of information bankers stock marketeers financial consultants lords of real estate and property developers and all their lawyers agents police and military makers and sellers of weapons lobbyists and go-betweens media and sports moguls popes and preachers and gurus professors and pundits business school faculty and the tycoons they spawned makers of plastic and fast food and bottled water

that's who they were not to mention my dentist whose son my teeth put through college they were the ones in the buBBles the ones who had refused or failed to stop the destruction of the planet who had profited from that destruction and then when the time came found safe haven when it was too late for the rest of us

droit au but

still we laboured on
in black harness and bells
in the department of lines
galley slaves rowing to the end cf the verse
hoppers spraying rhymes on the dance floor
all those lines are dead
dead and gone
dust in the stellar wind
organisms at the edge of life
deAdliNeRs

where dOctOr suZaNNe poNt-l'éVeQue went into
hiding now she'd dropped. out of the astronomical
industrial complex no one knew and still no one
knows did she find a leVeLLer camp somewhere out
in the outlands traded in her astrolabe and orrery for
trowel and watering can or maybe. gone alone into
the deadlands to live on fiddleheads and grass until
starvation or maybe suZaNNe poNt-l'éVeQue is
simply ensconced in a buBBle sipping dirty. martinis
by the pool

bObby 2shOes spots a large low adobe structure with several open windows peeking out from behind the common house so what's. in there co-care beTTy says bObby 2shOes moves away from his minders for a closer look where you dump your infected he guesses we take care of our sick bOOger rOOney corrects or kick them out into the desert bObby says beTTy shakes her head we don't do that but bObby 2shOes waves an arm. toward the east i've seen them wandering outside that bArNet camp the woman with the gun gives him a stone wall glare bArNet she says are not tRuE leVeLLers

taking up a position somewhere in northern latitudes and gazing in the direction of the nOrTh ecLiPtiC pOle an astronomer quickly discovers a diffuse blue-green disk crossed by an s-shaped brown curve with an intricate circular structure at the inner region she's looking. at the cAt's eYe nebula the core of the nebula has an apparent size of 50 cm and a high surface brightness

er. s'en allant promener
i was leaning on the railing on the starboard deck of
the evening ferry to gAliaNo island this was a long
time ago when the idea for a story came to me in the
form of a man coming up alongside this time of day
he said you sometimes see the orcas he was dressed
in casual. money in his fifties maybe with the grey
hair well. groomed look first time out here he asked i
nodded and making the effort conversation always
demands i asked him the same oh no he said i live on
the island lucky you i say his turn to nod i've got a
place on a promontory ocean views on three sides
mornings i step outside and into my kayak go for a
long. quiet paddle with the birds in a pristine
paradise wow i said sure does sound like paradise
have you lived there long two years now he replies
came out from alBerTa when i retired turns out he
was one of those oil company. executives who
polluted most of the globe and then spent their
millions on a retirement palace in one of the few
remaining clean natural havens on the planet

d'une manière très particulière
in the marketplace they were buying and selling
            lines of verse
meanwhile our work unit struggled to achieve
            our quota
so far we've failed to produce excellent
            praise-bait
praise that would shower down on
            our work
like ash and soot and the red sky
            to the south
who lay in this hospital bed i wonder before
            they scrubbed it down

behind the co-care hut a flat field. of cleared ground
stretches the length of a football pitch the graveyard
bObby guesses the field is clear of stones or crosses
to mark individual graves instead the names of the
dead are etched into a large boulder on the edge. of
the field we do green burials beTTy says no
cremation no coffins

the tRUe leVeLLers were the diehards the illuminated the ultra. orthodox the true believers work that is to say farming collecting twigs repairing their shacks composting all this was voluntary yet no one abstained they did not punish individual bad behaviour they sat the offender down for a circle talk they did not have meetings they held conversations they conducted check-ins and check-outs in which everyone took a turn celebrating the wonderful life of the group the tRUe leVeLLers refused the obvious that it was too late to save the planet the planet was fucked they were surrounded by and lived in a toxic and dangerous desert they were plagued by viruses and radioactive clouds and the fires to the south they had little or no water the rare rain that fell was poisoned they had no source of energy electric or chemical they shat in the sand and ate pale contaminated vegetables and yet they continued diligently recycling their rubbish burying their frequent dead in green funerals and refusing to consume meat in any form although the mutations of what animals. continued to roam the desert would make anyone reluctant. to eat them to some this stubborn refusal. to accept reality might seem admirable to the deAdliNeRs and also to bObby 2shOes it was plain stupid particularly since the bastards in the buBBles continued to dig for oil and mine for precious metals outside their buBBles abandoning the millions of creatures excluded from their safe havens to misery and a slow or less slow. death

and yet in spite of his disdain. for the leVeLLers and their illusionary community did some part of bObby 2shOes not feel an attraction to their world did their thinly veiled attempt to recruit him not tug ever so slightly at his heart was there still even now a longing. to belong

première parenthèse de l'auteur the author who finds themself outside the literary community excluded from the institutional dispositive of writing in their own country not to mention beyond in the wider world and not to mention the absence of a readership to what extent this exclusion is of their own doing their rejection of the shared norms and conventions of that community or rather the result of a refusal by that community to include the difference of their writing project the denial of their right to unexpected speech *le droit à la parole inattendue* or simply due to the poor quality of their writing i mean the possibility that they are just a bad writer all this is difficult to determine and certainly beyond the powers of the author's own judgement

quiconque

she was born to strangers
who were strangers to each other
and to themselves
on a planet that looped around a sun doomed
to burst and fade
in the long run towards the no future
where the past is never was

how long you figure your water. will last bObby 2shOes said once the buBBle bastards find it there beTTy shook her head you go dropping everyone in the same sentence she said like they're all alike what do you know about the buBBlers aside from how to kill them meanwhile a drone dropped below the layers of smoke in the sky and circled slowly above them best to get inside bOOger rOOney said

rumours about magic spells have been running round the outlands for some time where they come from what they can actually do no one can say for sure but spells have definitely been found and enough people have seen them to confirm the truth of their existence

auprès de ma blonde
note to my fellow blue and broken
your partners friends family cannot help you
you are an undeserved burden
and yet in the present historical moment
obscene contentment no
to survive blue and broken
without abandoning one's broken blues
a degree of solitude is probably essential

bObby 2shOes fighting the instinct. to run follows
bOOger rOOney into the common house the two
women. in the kitchen have been joined by three
more leVeLLers they're all wearing corona masks
now and standing awkwardly around as though in
expectation but of what rOOney goes over to fill
some cups. of berry juice brings one back to bObby
2shOes take a load off bObby 2shOes takes the drink
but prefers to stand rOOney sits in the first pew and
the other LeVeLLers on cue sit or turn back to their
kitchen work the room is silent beTTy bObby 2shOes
notices has disappeared

quatre-vingt cinq en conformiste
forms examined her
no formula could extricate her
she laboured under the influence
of her generation

A29
a few minutes passed the way time passes when you
think about it i mean slowly then beTTy reappeared
in the doorway she was carrying that rifle again but
loose in the crook of her arm nodded at bOOger who
got up turned to bObby 2shOes that squad of
yellowlegs he said. they're on the ground probably
best if you take off before they come in bObby
2shOes spun around the way you do when you're
looking for a quick exit this way beTTy said he
followed her out the door go round there she said
stepping back to let him by he turned back once
before turning the corner but she was already gone
back inside he ran low on bended knees along the
wall to the back where the yellowlegs were waiting
three of them their weapons not even drawn
expecting no. resistance

                    quatre-vingt cinq en maîtresse d'école
wipe away that tear babe
here come the soldiers of thought
ornamental verses
patriarchal decoration

                              quatre-vingt cinq humide
the examination followed us
up a river of influence
everything depends on influence
when you're addicted to family

                          quatre-vingt cinq moins neuf
on a low hanging branch
a watchful persimmon
appropriate to the situation
i mean to the poem

the spells seemed never to appear in the same place twice and in different forms sometimes on large. or small sheets of handmade paper sometimes. on birch bark or canvas and occasionally on small digital picture frames but some who'd found them swore. they had real power out near baReSHanKe a spell had reportedly brought three days of rain clean untainted water not all spells brought good fortune some. could bring harm and even death an outlander who'd attacked. a woman on the outskirts of bArNet. had drowned in a flash flood after finding a spell in his shack

quatre-vingt cinq comme un chien

how many before me
lying in this hospital bed
wrapped in these sheets
under the mountains in the window

nor did they get resistance oh no not from bObby
2shOes they didn't instead he slipped into. that
detached mode you enter under arrest when you've
lost all power over your body as though none of this
is happening to you which in the reader's case not to
mention the writer is certainly true the yellowlegs
were in full regalia helmets face and body shields and
those leggings they were no more human to him than
he was to them they spoke not a word and neither did
he which was to be expected they were the long arm.
of the law and he was the short end of the stick

quatre-vingt cinq zut alors

on a lifetime scholarship
of service to power
the sting of accidental family
rentals tests addiction

49

deuxième parenthèse de l'auteur we were travelling upriver on the caTuBig in nOrTHerN sAmaR in a pump-boat taxi powered by a small outboard motor that did the run regularly the river was wide enough up to one hundred metres in places but narrowing sometimes to less than twenty and winding so that you never knew what was around the corner

coLeTTe and i were seated in the stern just in front of the driver and his motor titO was up in the bow so that we were separated by a woman and her two small children and a couple of older men in t-shirts and jeans on their way home upriver from some work in town

we were headed to a small village not far from lAs nAvAs in the mountains ostensibly to visit a cooperative farm experimenting with species of corn and other vegetables for cultivation in hilly terrain but our real goal. was to make contact with the nPa guerrilla unit active in the area

tiTo was our guide he was maybe eighteen years old born in calBayOg cITy on the eastern coast of the island and he knew his way around which is important if you're working in the interzone before taking the boat he'd brought us to the mayor's house where we explained we were a kAnaDiAn research team with ciDA looking to set up economic and social projects in rural communities which was a lie the mayor served us an excellent lunch of escabeche which is pickled fried lapu-lapu fish and rice and gave his permission to go upriver

so we put that in our back pocket and headed out about three quarters of an hour along we came around a bend in the river and smack into a military outpost a couple of armed soldiers waving us over to the shore they were out of uniform in shorts and t-shirts

which was a worry because the military often moonlight as bandits and the less uniform the more banditry anyway the m-16s were real and our driver slowed and swerved to the landing a short scrappy pier

i thought about asking. him to make a run for it but that would have been unfair eventually he would have to come back this way so we came up along the pier two of the men on shore swung their rifles round their backs and took hold of the boat a third man appeared on the rise above the pier also in t-shirt shorts and flip-flops and sporting a goatee and a machete which was more of a worry than if he'd been carrying a rifle the military being occasionally fond of chopping off heads titO cast a quick glance back at us and began to stand to greet the man but i nodded him down and got up myself

the goatee and machete obviously the officer put one foot on the bow of the pump boat and gave me a wide grin what is it you are doing around here he asked something i was wondering myself at that moment we work for the kAnaDiAn government i lied he nodded human rights he said grinning you are human rights eh

i shook my head we're looking for investment opportunities here in sAmaR if its right we'll bring in lots of money he shrugged held out his hand passports

i caught titO looking back at me trying to decide how i was doing if he should intervene i dug my passport out of my pocket waved it at the machete man see i said kAnaDiAn passport he gestured to hand it over but i stuffed it back in my pocket everything is arranged i said with his hOnOUr mAyoR paDuaNO he'll be angry i said if we have trouble you know paDuaNO i said and he nodded slowly studying me still grinning but not so sure now

i could feel the tension in the boat everyone sitting very still very quiet i took a chance what's your name and rank i said his grin vanished you step out he said come up to camp we'll make a check it will be okay

coLeTTe produced a sigh as though this was all taking too long i took a quick peek back at her and she was looking at her watch lips pursed no sign of fear doing her best imitation of the white tourist

i took the cue shook my head no i said you check with the mAyoR send someone you're not busy here we're moving on i turned to the driver let's go he looked from me to the officer and back let's go i repeated and sat down the officer kept a glare on me but he straightened and pushed at the bow of the pump boat with his foot the driver started up his motor and reversed back into the river

à l'envers

clouded mind my left hand on
the garden gate of two minds

astrolabe the universe in my other hand what
gender what genre gathered in the house

of wisdom now we are all that masked
individual and isn't it time we rethought

those categories those historical periods
middle ages age of discovery classical antiquity
isLaMiC golden age last tUesDaY
late victorian little bObby 2shOes

in the porkchopper they had him down on his knees
so that he only caught a glimpse of the desert then the
grey metallic mountains separating. the abandoned
from the coastal buBBles he closed his eyes to go
elsewhere in his head back to the time with the
deAdliNeRs west of baReSHanKe

they were a small pack mostly taking pot shots at passing transports from the rare-earth metal mines out in the desert maybe slowing. the supply chain a bit in the outlands they were called the neoDime not because they dealt in some new currency but on account of the rare-earth metals in the area neodymium some dysprosium and cerium some mixed in with lithium

the neoDime deAdliNeRs moved around a lot slept under scavenged tarps quick to put up and take down hiding from the drones under the flimsy canopies of the remnants of dOuGlaS firs the pack was mostly ex-oil workers some foreign. labourers brought in and then cast aside some men and women from the dark-skinned ghettoes who'd lost their jobs to the eco-shift their homes to the banks their families to disease and despair also a few liberal arts intellectuals who the bubble had no use for and who didn't tend to last long out in the outland

patates frites
if a failed musician can nevertheless play for zirself
can't a forgotten poet write lines of verse for zirself
in a dead language
the end of the world as zir only deadline
deadlocked deadpan deadhead deadbeat dreadlocks
dead letter dead hand dead loss dead weight dead end

en dansant le long des golfes clairs
they were tattered scraps of paper
the leftovers of her lost archive
huBBle's long gaze at a dying star
a thousand years old
the cat's returning gaze

she cut and burned the edges
inscribed a magic spell
to change the world

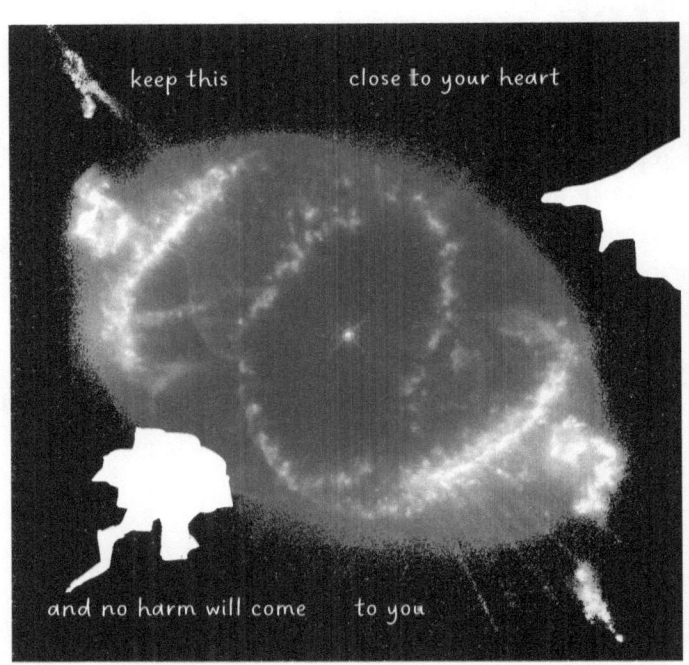

for his part bObby 2shOes had neither job skills nor education he'd been an outlander from the start born into it his only weapons fear and fast feet because the only way to get a firearm was to take it from a yellowlegs which ♫ had done because ze carried an m4A7 carbine and taught bObby how to shoot ♫ kept mostly to zirself but. ze let bObby 2shOes practise sighting a target without actually shooting cartridges being hard to come by why ♫ even gave him the time when ze would barely talk to the other deAdliNeRs he couldn't figure maybe because he made the effort to learn zir pronouns

Resolved — to Plant and Manure the Waste land
upon George-Hill in the parish of Walton
in the county of Surrey

plenty of rumours. circulating about the whereabouts of dOctOr suZaNNe poNt-l'éVeQue some claimed they'd seen a solitary shelter miles outside the bArNet leVeLLers' camp maybe bArNet were supplying her with food water oil paints and felt pens in exchange for her spells these were merely rumours unsubstantiated. and fuelled by a widespread dislike. of bArNet their treatment of the old and infirm outcasts and migrants seeking shelter not to mention their relative wealth compared to other leVeLLer camps never mind deAdliNeRs

why he'd been too shy when he had the chance that question all the more painful. now as he kneeled in the belly of the porkchopper knowing the chance was almost certainly gone forever if it had ever existed ♪♪ had never given him the slightest hint ze shared any such feelings in fact the whole time he'd hung with the neoDime ♪♪ had shown no affection toward him or any of the others actually ze'd shown no feelings at all. hard as nails was ♪♪

the hUbbLe sPacE teLeScOpe reveals
knots jets bubbles arcs
surrounding and illuminated
by a central hot
planetary nebula nucleus

comme un homme blanc

what remains
only what blaNchOt claimed
le droit à la parole inattendue

which is why. he could only go
from disappointment
to disappointment

somewhere above the iron peaks of the mountains bordering the buBBle one of the yellowlegs slid the chopper hatch open the other two dragged bObby 2shOes along the floor to the open door and pitched him out into the sky you can imagine the rest

well maybe you prefer not to imagine. the long fall to almost certain death well really it's certain but i wrote almost because of the difficulty of imagining. one's own death anyway the rush of air as you leave the whirlybird a glimpse of the earth below before the wind begins to twirl you pulling and twisting your arms and legs your head swooning let's try to stop spinning spreadeagle those arms and legs this slows you down gets you sailing and swooping now watch the earth vaguely brown darkly rising towards you beckoning oh look what i've done i've killed my protagonist and i did it purely. on a whim it came to me like that unbidden slid past the censor that lurks deep in the author's imagination luckily even now. as the author of this sordid farce i can quickly rectify my impulse and pull bObby 2shOes back up into the porkchop and onto his knees in order that the story might continue though where it's headed is unclear brown ground darkly rising towards us beckoning

And that this Civil Propriety is the Curse, is manifest thus, Those that Buy and Sell Land, and are landlords, have got it either by Oppression, or Murther, or Theft; and all landlords live in the breach of the Seventh and Eighth Commandments, Thou shalt not steal, or kill.

The True Levellers Standard Advanced: or The State of Community opened, and Presented to the Sons of Men
— Gerrard Winstanley, 1649

following in the footsteps of deːLef scHönBerneR
dOctOr suZaNNe poNt-l'éVeQue's work
had been to trace the evolutionary track of
the central star of NGC 6543
toward becoming a white dwarf and
to its ultimate fate

                                        à marée basse
the occasional sound of small floatplanes
winters being mild
geese do not fly south directly
at some set and recurrent seasonal time
but rather drift back and forth as the temperature
fluctuates
heading south on cold days
and northward when it warms
their triangular echelons cross and recross
this patch of sky
turning heads one way then the other
whereas in colder climes
heads turn one way throughout the fall and
back the other way in springtime

of course those yellowlegs didn't toss bObby 2shOes from the porkchopper that would be very poor plotting they were merely. amusing themselves as any red blooded yellowlegs will do dangling their prisoner. over the edge of the hatch for a few entertaining moments kid pissed himself one yellowlegs announced with a chuckle

the speed of light = 300 million metres per second
a light year = 9.5 trillion kms or 5.9 trillion miles
a megaparsec = 3.2 million light-years
a star 10 light-years away is 10 years in the past
from our perspective

once golden cities now ghost towns
once green fields now parched cracked empty

to quench your thirst drink oil
your children are coming
to murder you in your beds

du fond de la ruelle

reading a book entitled my ugly shoes
the sun on my face and
my ugly shoes

although traffic is light it will take forever
all thou terrifically slight and wilted aches and fever
didn't i dust and sweep and polish
because cleaning house entitled my ugly shoes

when i am weary of these aches and fever
weary of the dust and polish
i gaze upon my ugly shoes
which is a consolation

but i've already written about this
about my aches and fever and my ugly shoes
i've already written about this

and yet

isn't reiteration
even regarding ugly footwear
sometimes a consolation

eventually. those rollicking yellowlegs pulled bObby
2shOes back into the whirlybird and onto his knees
but not before. the chopper had cleared the
mountains the sky turned blue and bObby caught a
bird's eye. of the border fence the fields of wind.
turbines and the city in a buBBle

à marée haute

writing is done by breathing
the inhalation gathers all that is myself
including the immediate troposphere
wherein i am enfolded

then follows the exhalation of all that self
and the inhalation of another self
to become little bObby 2shOes
and all the air that enwraps him

i and maybe you might imagine the city in the buBBle as some futuristic ultra sci-fi duBAi-times-ten with glittering higher than high-rises shaped like globes bows doughnuts and top hats with green high lines the size of boulevards all beneath flying cars and beam-me-up-scotties but. that's not how things happened oh sure lots of drones and choppers the occasional e-jumbo jet crisscrossing above the city and plenty of high rises though architecturally restrained and covered in green but really this buBBle city looks much the way it did in the early 21st century along with many of the environmental corrections we hoped. the world would adopt so lots of solar paneled roofs electric powered vehicles more public transport more pedestrian walkways and green spaces the problem. of course being that all these improvements came too late for 90% of the planet and the cost of living in the buBBles especially real estate and food prices drove the majority of humans out and into the parched and poisoned outlands

maybe you is any writer's idea of an audience

And such as there rise up to be rich in the objects of the
Earth; then by their plausible words of flattery to the plain-
hearted people, whom they deceive, and that lies under
confusion and blindness: They are lifted up to be Teachers,
Rulers and Law makers over them that lifted them up; as
if the Earth were made peculiarly for them, and not for
others weal

the inFoRmaTioN couNciL for the enVirOnmeNT
wants to know if the eARTh is getting warmer why is
kEntuCkY getting colder

encircling the centre of the cAt's eYe nebula are
eleven concentric rings these rings were created by
pulsations emitted by the progenitor star during a
period beginning 15,000 years ago and ending 1000
years ago when the core of the nebula was formed

in a few million years the cAt's eYe nebula
will collapse into a white dwarf

bObby in the buBBle they left him in a windowless
cell windowless maybe but not a dungeon as you
might imagine as though i had the slightest idea
what. you might imagine let's leave the reader to zir
own imagination they taught me the author should
leave most things to the reader's imagination trouble
is i can barely imagine. a reader but back to the
dungeon it was not a dungeon rather a small clean
well lighted pale green room with a porcelain toilet
and sink and a low built-in shelf upon which lay a
pallet somewhere between a yoga mat and a futon
and of course a door complete with. spyhole anyway
digression is merely another form of narrative

comme des garçons
metastability the momentary stability
a kind of false or temporary but doomed stability
a deAdliNer travels in the mycorrhizal networks
of zir imagination
because justice does not wait
it comes in an instant of decision
a moment of madness

whatever destruction humans reap on their home planet in the short term. the sun will most likely end in similar fashion to the cAt's eYe nebula in about five billion years first expanding into a red giant 100 times its actual diameter before expelling its outer layers into. space by then all the plays and poems of wiLLiAm sHakeSpeaRe not to mention my own will be lost forever hence the futility of striving for fame this did not deter suZaNNe poNt-l'éVeQue from the desire to prolong the life of her planet in spite of her and my and possibly your powerlessness but she waged this struggle without expectation. of reward and in the pride and magic. of anonymity

comme un pied de nez

the most serious problem with catastrophic global warming is it may not be true — ICE (inFoRmaTioN couNciL for the enVirOnmeNT) an organization dedicated to repositioning global warming as theory not fact

the right side of ♪'s head was shaved with a looped
chain in zir ear the left side was a long black braid ze
wore a nose ring a woollen turtleneck and tattered
denim bellbottoms and like bObby 2shOes ♪ was
barefoot he remembered ♪'s implacable brown toes

suZaNNe would not allow the finitude
of existence to defeat her

accepting the planet's inevitable destruction she
thought might release us* from ambition's strife

in our few remaining years
we might simply get along
lend a hand share a meal

let poems wash over us*
and vanish like water on a stone

*by us and we here i mean living creatures fauna
and flora also stones because stones are people too
even though they do not bother with birth and
death and everything in-between

allongé

if they left him in that cell a. long. time it was not part of a strategy to break. him down but they were busy with more important matters result it took a while before they got around to bObby 2shOes and their plans for him because they did. have plans. for him

these are the ones to stay away from those who enjoy teaching and believe they are good at it all those with values they can list and carry around in their hip pockets neophytes proselytizers of every stripe those who used to smoke snort or shoot up and won't tolerate those who still do the eternal optimists those who know exactly how you feel academics who chose the management side those who would buy or sell your home anyone that wants 10% of what you've created those who don't want anything you've created those who rise early bright eyed and bushy tailed those who have a great idea for a movie those who have great ideas those who have no idea

sans pitié

the poem is a small black squirrel that leaps
from the tree branch to the roof
but no not the small black squirrel but the leaping
of the small black squirrel
from the tree branch to the roof

the poem is the event of that small black squirrel.
leaping. the event of the leaping and my presence
gazing on the leaping. possibly the poem is merely
this sentence. its leaping and gazing roofing and
squirrelling

a perturbation is a small disturbance which makes
the system deviate from its state of equilibrium any
system that does not return to its equilibrium after a
perturbation is deemed unstable

a couple of yellowlegs came for him in his cell marched him up the back stairs down a long corridor to the room of questions and bObby 2shOes certainly had plenty. of questions but those were not the questions for which that room was intended his questions remained where they were in his throat the room itself was clean pale green walls a large wooden table coated in a kind of thermoplastic with three folding chairs two with their backs to the door and one on the far side facing the door the room was not especially intimidating no see-through mirror no blood on the walls no gauges across the tabletop no pools of undefined liquid on the floor the only vaguely troubling thing. was a white porcelain sink in the corner

contre le courant

whenever they spoke the word *we*
ze heard the words *not them*

it wasn't a case of an astrophysicist turning. away from science and into a kind of magical thinking because recosmicizing was not magical thinking the stars were still stars luminous spheroids of plasma and galaxies were gravitationally bound systems of stars and gas and dust but the stars were also divine guardians dancing in paradise the galaxies were angels' wings dOctOr suZaNNe poNt-l'éVeQue had found a way. to hold both sets of knowledge in the palm of her mind without falling into the straight jacket of cognitive dissonance she had become a cosmological dAOist manufacturing her spells under the brilliant gaze of the cAt's eYe nebula

It was shewed us by Vision in Dreams, and out of Dreams, That that should be the Place we should begin upon. And though that Earth in view of Flesh, be very barren, yet we should trust the Spirit for a blessing.

possible ways the universe will come to an end
(1) HEAT DEATH in which the universe expands
until everything is further and further apart so that
the universe eventually becomes cold dark and
empty

de travers

the false nine explained
because writing turns out to be a kind of suicide
to be briefly other than my self
the way a squall sweeps through the harbour
afterwards the air cleansed
my face wet

they let him sit and stew. in that room a while pale green walls thermoplasticized oak table folding chairs and that oddly menacing sink in one corner time for a long think but not much to think about because. it was all out of his hands now all his life scratching and clawing for a mouthful and a place to lie down he felt relief mostly the relief at the end of the struggle because really sooner or later. what other outcome could he have expected so relief rather than fear well a bit of fear thinking where would they put him or bury him but relief mostly followed by a wave. of fatigue. washing over him a wave so powerful that his eyelids dropped and he lay his head down. on the thermoplasticized table

what wakes him up is the needle in his arm a yellowlegs pathomask face shield hovering above him for a split second bObby 2shOes thinks maybe. the guy's injecting something unpleasant he waits for the taste of poison but no the yellowlegs is just sucking bObby's blood bObby sits up to watch the guy remove the syringe fire a digital thermometer at bObby 2shOes's forehead and leave the room after that they let him sit. and stew. a while longer

shTicK giltGesTaLt's head is big and hairless and his complexion like that of most buBBlers except those who frequent the tanning parlours is very white he's wearing a dark turtle neck track suit on a pear-shaped body so that he looks to bObby like a dressed-up snowman but the roly-poly look is offset by a lot of high tech accessories AR glasses silver ear pods and a smart watch but no pathomask so bObby 2shOes figures his recent blood test must have come back low on the transmissibility scale shTicK giltGesTaLt sits down on the power. side of the thermoplasticized table and studies 2shOes through his smart glasses for a moment

chez le dentiste

bObby 2shOes tries to focus on the door. behind giltGesTaLt to avoid the gaze behind. those glasses because the interrogator is looking at him but looking at lots of AR stuff at the same time so that he's both looking and not looking the questions when they finally come are delivered. in a high alto choirboy's voice so that they seem more like innocent curiosity than the prelude to some form of torture

when did you join the deAdliNeRs i'm not a deAdliNeR bObby 2shOes says to the door a slight pause. as shTicK giltGesTaLt consults a file somewhere in the air above the table between them and visible only to him before moving on to the next question

oh but weren't you running with the gang they call the neoDime i'm not a deAdliNeR a nod from shTicK giltGesTaLt oh and were you in bArNet for a long time what was that like i'm not a leVeLLer

impersonnel

so when you saw them expel a woman carrying the omega virus into the desert you were out there. with titO's pack of deAdliNeRs you were maybe not a deAdliNeR but out there with them

well that brought back memories titO of course their de facto leader and the band and 𝅘𝅥𝅮𝅘𝅥𝅮 furious at titO and the others because they refused. to help the sick one so what if the woman was a leVeLLer 𝅘𝅥𝅮𝅘𝅥𝅮 argued she wasn't a leVeLLer now angry at bObby too for keeping out of it imitating him but making it sound whiny i'm not a deAdliNeR in the end 𝅘𝅥𝅮𝅘𝅥𝅮 had gone to the woman shared zir precious. water oblivious to the virus

and you were in the area at the time of the atmospheric river and the bArNet floods shTicK giltGesTaLt says reading off his invisible. file and interrupting bObby 2shOes's reverie so you're aware a leVeLLer drowned *de mauvais goût*

now shTicK pressing his preponderance against the edge of the table to reduce the distance. between them then perhaps he says you heard talk at the time about a magic spell bObby 2shOes shrugs oh well never mind giltGesTaLt says matching bObby's shrug with one of his own all so much superstitious twattle

i wonder shTicK giltGesTaLt whispers in a tone unfamiliar to bObby 2shOes but which he suspects is intended to be kindly do you have any. family anywhere then in the face of bObby's blank face no i suppose not so this is the first time you've been in the grEEn beLt well first we better get you a pair of shoes

when and with which of his gadgets glasses watch or ear pods shTicK giltGesTaLt summoned jOeY caFgU remains a mystery. to bObby 2shOes but suddenly jOeY caFgU is handing him a pair of thick-soled electric blue brothel creepers the size is right but bObby's feet feel strangely confined in shoes and when he straightens up shTicK giltGesTaLt is gone

léthargique

the story progressing slowly
just to feel the rattle of house keys
between my fingers
outside they're drilling teeth in the street

birth is a falling from a great height
too dizzy to figure out the world
before momentum and gravity carry you
down to the end of the verse

any fiction is mostly a terrifying reduction of the real

possible ways the universe will come to an end
(2) THE BIG RIP wherein dark energy turns out to
be a phantom energy that grows over time not just
moving galaxies further and further apart but tearing
everything apart in other words you can't hide from
space

terraforming or the process by which humans make distant planets suitable for human habitation

The solar system is ours, let's take it.
                                          — James Green
         diRector of nAsA's plaNetARy scIenCe diViSioN

For it is shewed us, That so long as we, or any other, doth own the Earth to be the peculiar Interest of Lords and Landlords, and not common to others as well as them, we own the Curse, and hold the Creation under bondage; and so long as we or any other doth own Landlords and Tennants, for one to call the Land his, or another to hire it of him, or for one to give hire, and for another to work for hire; this is to dishonour the work of Creation; as if the righteous Creator should have respect to persons, and therefore made the Earth for some, and not for all

we know from past adventures in another universe.
between the covers that jOeY caFgU was a tight-
lipped fellow though he'd occasionally let his hands
do the talking nevertheless clearly his assigned task
was to take bObby 2shOes who was now in shoes on
a tour. of the buBBle they left the prison house of law
and order by a side door which was better than
leaving via the underground garage through which
bObby 2shOes without shoes had been brought in

                                        langue de bois
in the morning red sky pouring slate
cough and cling to a crumbling shoreline
belly up fish distant sound of rockets

in the morning science told the world
we have to stop pumping greenhouse gases
into the atmosphere

the poli-petro-bankers replied
science does not tell us what to do
we tell science what to do

troisième parenthèse de l'auteur
—;!
thoughts on the novel entitled —;!
at first glance —;! appears to be no different from any conventional novel a beginning a middle and an end in that order but there is a difficulty because —;! is at once the title of the novel the name of the main and sole character and the entire text of the novel

at the very least the author might have used actual words instead of punctuation marks they might have named the character dash-semi-colon-exclamation-mark they might have assigned some physical attributes to —;! tight black curls a thin long frame long delicate hands unfortunately in this case what you see is pretty much what you get —;!

the idea that —;! might be a character flies in the face of everything we know about the art of fiction and yet undeniably —;! is unique no jaCK or jiLL here what we have is a combination in a particular order of signs you won't find in another text because in all of fiction no character has ever been named —;!

an added advantage is that a character composed entirely of punctuation marks needs no translation into a great number of languages with notable exceptions such as the scriptio continua in the tOrAh or lAtiN or traditional cHinEsE or jApaNeSe

but what if anything can be said of the character —;! on closer examination something of the personality of —;! does emerge we discover a long pause in some sort of causal relation with an emphatic exclamation almost as though a long process of patient thought has suddenly taken us to a stunning conclusion there is movement here a kind of reflexive delay erupting into revelatory action we might even imagine in the preceding long dash a shade of the father's ghost

so what we have here is not only a character but simultaneously a kind of action the actual plot of the story and we know that in fiction character is really defined by plot any character is nothing more than what he or she does or doesn't do in that sense —;! is possibly the quintessential story a narrative in which character and plot are one and the same the atmosphere in —;! might be described as a combination of mystery and great simplicity we have so far been interpreting the exclamation mark as a sign of triumph eureka however ! could just as easily denote some horrifying realization is this the sudden discovery of our sister's body buried in the crypt or the master's wife declared mad and imprisoned in the attic

turning our attention to crisis because we've been told that narrative must culminate in some sort of crisis and —;! does exactly that as the apex of the fichtean curve in —;! is located precisely between the semicolon and the exclamation mark admittedly there follows not much of a denouement but the story resonates in the mind long after we have put it down we have not forgotten that all meaning in the best fiction as per wiLLiAm fAulKneR comes from the heart in conflict with itself although this obviously applies more to a privileged white world than to one in which characters struggle to free themselves from under that white man's boot stories in which the conflict is between oppressed and oppressor but I digress and there's no place I've been told in an essay for digression at first glance —;! might appear to be nothing more than a rip-roaring adventure devoid of theme certainly the exclamation mark invites such a reading but the long dash which introduces the story complicates the issue evoking an inner struggle and a contemplative nature the drawn-out struggle over whether to avenge or not to avenge the ghost and the semicolon is crucial appearing at the very heart of the story because of all punctuation marks the semicolon is clearly the most difficult and the most complex indicating both a relation of causality and contradiction so that in the semi-colon is contained a process so fundamental to a way of thinking linear rational logical dialectic based on reason which suggests that in the end more than a simple narrative —;! represents and unmasks the way the rising curve of the classic narrative structure rests squarely on the wEstErN metaphysical tradition which we know by now is not universal thus in —;! we have a work that contains within three commonplace signs its own title character atmosphere and plot as well as a satirical rehearsal of a chRistIaN platonic world view and yes its own critical discussion at last a book you can tell by its cover and proof that punctuation without words is all you need to tell a story

possible ways the universe will come to an end
(3) VACUUM DECAY or the spontaneous appearance of a quantum bubble of death that grows and grows and devours the universe or what happens when physics breaks

out in the street and looking back bObby 2shOes with shoes was surprised to see the prison house of law and order was only three floors high most of it he realized must be underground underground is where secrets and. death not to mention death's secrets are best located the front façade of the building was mostly glass panes the angled roof covered in solar panels and topped with a row of three tall wind cowls the hoods of which were brightly coloured orange green and pink and turning for a panorama bObby 2shOes with shoes discovered as far as he could see both sides of the boulevard were lined with identical houses three stories glass solar panels and variously coloured wind cowls the middle of the street was a pedestrian rambla two lanes wide with bicycle lanes running along both sides and two single lanes of cars on either side of these the cars were silent driverless aerodynamic bubbles the interiors looking more like sitting rooms than vehicles some of them carried. no passengers

comme un steak frites

still we struggle under the weight
of these dead lines

the red sky
the fires to the south

turns out a dead line is so much heavier
than a lively rhyme

even our wings could not lift us
anywhere close to the sun

close the book
the cover tells you everything you need to know

They have by their subtle imaginary and covetous wit,
got the plain-hearted poor, or yonger Brethren to work
for them, for small wages, and by their work have got a
great increase; for the poor by their labour lifts up
Tyrants to rule over them; or else by their covetous wit,
they have out-reached the plain-hearted in Buying and
Selling, and thereby inriched themselves, but
impoverished others: or else by their subtile wit, having
been a lifter up into places of Trust, have inforced people
to pay Money for a Publick use, but have divided much of
it into their private purses; and so have got it by
Oppression.

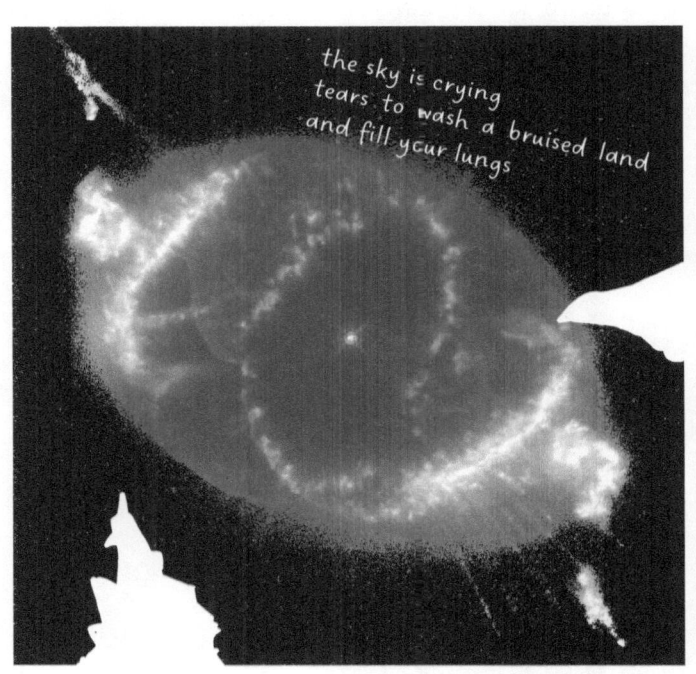

the sky is crying
tears to wash a bruised land
and fill your lungs

étonné

several men sitting at a cafe terrace on the rambla dressed in leisure suits and trainers and equipped with those smart. glasses like shTicK giltGesTaLt's bObby 2shOes with shoes can't quite make out what language. they're speaking so straining to hear something of their conversation when he's squeezed out of his tourist gawking by jOeY caFgU's grip on his elbow

the anDroMedA galaxy a great spiral disk of a trillion stars spinning around a massive black hole and hurtling toward eArTh at 110 kilometres per second get ready in about four billion years anDroMedA and our miLkY wAy galaxy will collide jOeY caFgU the reader may recall reading in an earlier volume or not there may not even be a reader the reader is located in a space-time continuum that is unavailable to the author except as a mathematical quantum equation whereas the writer appears to the reader as a supernova already long. gone hello reader are you there but i digress i only meant to say jOeY caFgU was shTicK giltGesTaLt's golem shorter than bObby 2shOes with or without. shoes and squat with a wrestler's neck bObby 2shOes with shoes knew better than to get into a punch up with a golem nevertheless he managed a consolation. via a backward stumble to grind an innocent. heel into jOeY caFgU's toe alas unmoved jOeY dismissed this pale attempt at violence with an eye roll and a head shake and shoved bObby 2shOes with shoes along the narrow sidewalk toward the corner

she used huBBle's law $v = H_0D$ to calculate the distance between herself and her colleagues and the speed at which they were moving away from her

there were no street lights or stop signs on the corner nor as far as he could see the cars were somehow able to communicate and moderate their speeds so that they weaved in and out and past each other the boulevard was a river with occasional cross currents jOeY caFgU paused to allow bObby 2shOes standing in two shoes time to take it all. in

entre deux joints

1953 ameriKan toBaCCo coMPaNy creates toBaCCo inDustRy reSearCH coMMiTTee (tIrC)

1989 tIrC launches pRojEct whItEcoAt to reverse scientific and popular view that smoking is harmful and to restore social acceptability of smoking

1989 energy companies and fossil fuel dependent industries form the gLobAL cLiMatE coaLiTioN to lobby aMeriKan politicians and media

1991 the eDiSOn eLecTriC iNsTitUte a trade body representing electrical companies in the usA launched the inForMaTioN couNciL for the enViRonMent (iCe) campaign to reposition global warming as theory rather than fact

the rambla here became a vegetable garden and fruit orchard and as bObby 2shOes with shoes gazed transfixed at all the greenery a hidden sprinkler system suddenly erupted in a fine spray of precious water while in the blue sky above them silent drones darted some carrying packages others merely. observing

la main gauche sur les couilles à la micHaEl jaCksOn
zir name was ♪♪
because the other is not my alter ego
not the other outside of my self
not the other within my self

the assassinations began. during the chaos of the
mItIgaTioN period before the buBBle boundaries
were militarized and passports introduced

the first targets were the world. leaders attending
cOp57 ten thousand girls and women had changed
their names to gReTA and descended on ulAAn
bAAtAr where the politicians had hoped to escape
the crowds anyway the latter were dwindling by then
even the staunchest ecowarriors had grown weary of
marching in the streets the political and corporate
gangsters oil barons clear cutters coal diggers carbon
fuellers etc having discovered that a constant stream
of climate summits would eventually wear down
protesters at that time the list of cOp57 participants
began to appear on wanted posters then during the
final photo op. of cOp57 a deAdliNeR passing as a
touchup makeup artist stabbed the ameriKan
president in the throat the president lay down on the
green-washed stage and bled to death before the
emergency medics could get through the crowd of
uppity-ups and attending sycophants

comme un hors-d'œuvre

zir name was ♪♫
you could not argue with zir
ze had a mind like a dishrack
any new theory came along
ze'd just stack it up alongside the others
and let it drip dry

zir's was a theory of knots and bits of string
school of minnows house of sparrows
tangle of eelgrass
wood chips pencil shavings paper cuts

a **redshift** measured as 0 indicates the local present-
day universe
if the redshift observed in a distant cosmic object
say a galaxy or a supernova is 1 that object is seven
billion years ago
therefore if the redshift observed is negative the
object is in the future

In that we begin to Digge upon George-Hill, to eate our Bread together by righteous labour, and sweat of our browes... And that not only this Common, or Heath should be taken in and Manured by the People, but all the Commons and waste Ground in England and in the whole World, shall be taken in by the People in righteousness, not owning any Propriety; but taking the Earth to be a Common Treasury, as it was first made for all

a passing chopper ripped the silence bObby 2shOes with shoes turned to jOeY caFgU where're we going a question the reader not to mention. the writer might ask but jOeY didn't bother to answer instead he tapped his watch and a passing car glided to a stop the gullwing door of the car whooshing up to reveal a circle of cushioned seating surrounding a hologram of a map git in jOeY said which they did and the car slipped back. into the traffic

entre guillemets

for a while the white world claimed that all human endeavour could be divided into three basic categories art science and commerce then science and art were subsumed in the service of commerce then science became commerce and art became commerce

the white hen the red wheelbarrow the rain

the central star had expelled its mass in a series of pulses occurring at 1500-year intervals creating concentric shells of dust around the dying central star in her work dOctOr suZaNNe poNt-l'éVeQue was unhurried she ignored. the pressure to publish she knew that the cAt's eYe nebula would gradually disperse over several. thousand. years. as for the progenitor star it would eventually cool down to become a white dwarf not unlike suZaNNe's father the music in the car was jOhn cAgE's 44 haRMoNies which. coincidentally is what the author is listening to at this moment of writing but let's imagine they rode through the city centre glass towers backlit screens powered by volumes of solar panels advertising molybdenum bracelets smart glasses t-shirts e-sweatpants anything that cost money mannequins in storefront windows decked out in everything that would be useless in the outlands boutiques full of swank glimpses of baseball bat sized breads wagon-wheels of soft cheese double-decker frothy cakes a forest of asparagus pyramids of incandescent apples

dans la langue de l'Autre

thoughts on mitigation
没有将来

except. for those sipping lattes in the rambla terraces the people downtown were scuttling in and out of cars fast-walking to and from work or shopping dressed casual some in vaguely circus-y clothes some in artsy black they were almost all in gym workout shape and enveloped in slightly opaque electromagnetic fog due to all the e-gear they were sporting meanwhile. the sky had clouded over and a faint drizzle began to fall

avec un certain recul

because the death of the other
exposes the subject
to a finitude
the courtship of A5591 and 61991

astrophysicists agree the universe or at least the one we live in because there may very well be others in any case on this they do agree that based on observational evidence this universe is expanding at an increasingly rapid rate although what causes this accelerated expansion is unclear it must be a force opposite to and stronger than gravity a force that repels rather than attracts cosmic bodies

this hypothetical and invisible force has been dubbed dark energy and it is responsible for the accelerating expansion of the universe which necessarily creates more. and. more empty space between and within the approximately 125 billion galaxies (1.25×10^{11}) the black holes supernovas and all cosmic matter and more empty space results in more dark energy which in turn causes more expansion more emptiness more dark energy and on and on until the stars have burned out all cosmic particles have decayed all the black holes have evaporated and the universe this one anyway is a dark and empty void

a disembodied voice interrupted the music in the car
due to dangerous precipitation the voice said do not
exit the vehicle at this. time the holo-screen flashed
the same warning in several languages and bObby
2shOes with shoes heard the click of the car doors
locking automatically outside people raced for cover
large metallic parasols blossomed. over the terraces
on the rambla and the clients huddled beneath them
bObby 2shOes with shoes's eyes began to water and
a powerful sulphurous smell filled the vehicle the
drizzle became rain a rain that pounded the road and
pedestrian surfaces into a yellow foam

en y regardant à deux fois

meanwhile ten minutes earlier
ginger tea
harbour seals lounge among the rocks
a bird in black perched atop bada shanren's brush
bits of string leafless branches a stone
the housing market green tech
the pencil shavings of a life
i was only ever a hat on a street corner

Informeth, that on Sunday was seen night last, there was one Everard, once of the army but was cashiered, who termeth himself a prophet, one Stewer and Colten, and two more, all living at Cobham, came to St. George's Hill in Surrey, and began to dig on that side the hill next to Campe Close, and sowed the ground with parsnips, carrots, and beans. On Monday following they were there again, increased in their number, and on the next day, being Tuesday, they fired the heath, and burned at least forty rood of heath, which is a very great prejudice to the town. On Friday last they came again, and wrought all day at digging. They did then intend to have two or three ploughs at work, but they had not furnished themselves with seed-corn, which they did on Saturday. They invite all to come in and help them, and promise them meat, drink, and clothes. They do threaten to pull down and level all park pales, and intend to plant there very shortly. They say they will be four or five thousand within ten days, and threaten the neighbouring people that they will make them all come up to the hills and work: and forewarn them suffering their cattle to come near the plantation; if they do, they will cut their legs off. It is feared they have some design in hand.

- Henry Sanders, 16 April 1649

avec anticipation

a traveller said
stand in the desert stand on the sand
a shattered frown a wrinkled lip
the passion of lifeless things a hand a heart
on the pedestal of despair
sand stretching wherever the eye can see
nothing beside remains

sand legs of stone a shattered visage things

suZaNNe poNt-l'éVeQue had learned to gaze into
the growing emptiness of space without flinching she
carried the inevitable end of the universe as well as
her own lightly it did not keep her from making her
bed in the morning and taking the time to learn to
bake an upside down pineapple cake she took the
same care and time with a quantum equation or
painting a magic spell

over time a long long time
the question remains
i do this i do that
still the question remains

not to be vulnerable not to appeal for this or that
not to rely on this or that
to work hard nose to the grindstone

or to be modern instead
to cut paths take shortcuts
still the question remains

our disastrous ways of living
oh well never mind nothing lasts for ever
do this do that

over time a mere handful of billion years
all those acid-free libraries michelangelo's ceiling
the danyang-kunshan grand bridge
the james webb telescope
this book is a cosmic eschatology
because the ultimate goal of science
is to prepare for the death of the sun
and that's true of poetry as well

sur la pointe des pieds
the rain passed as all things do 'cept when they don't
and the car set off. again a breeze of sanitized air
streaming out of vents in the roof and expelling the
rain's rotten breath people stepped out of their
shelters and the streets filled up everything rolling
again after a while they left the city centre the road
became a highway wide and slick running past hi-
tech factories and green fields of corn alfalfa
tomatoes potatoes under fountains of arcing water
where are we going bObby 2shOes with shoes asked.
again jOeY caFgU just pointed toward the horizon
bObby 2shOes with shoes peering through the
window saw a long rocket rising toward the heavens
on a column of white smoke

comme une omelette
the nanLing mountains in southern cHiNa contain
half the world's tungsten deposits cHiNese mining
companies also produce tungsten as a byproduct of
the refining process for rare-earth metals like
molybdenum

cApE mUsK stretches over several hundred acres shTicK giltGesTaLt is already there waiting to personally give bObby 2shOes with shoes the tour there are multiple runways hangars and helipads but the main attraction. is a fully equipped spaceport including three launchpads on two of which sit rockets wrapped in scaffolding and swarming with personnel this shTicK tells bObby 2shOes with shoes is sTaTioN nEw eArtH our repository of the past our mitigation of present threats and our door to the future

according to the ekpyrotic scenario for the origin and fate of the cosmos our universe is just one of several 3-dimensional branes or universes within a higher-dimensional space in which gravity but nothing else can travel ekpyrotic comes from the Greek word for conflagration the theory being. that our particular universe appeared as a result of an explosion caused by the collision of two other universes

we have six of these reusable rockets and we launch twice a week the rockets' first task is to release sulfur dioxide into the stratosphere where it combines with water to create a haze. of tiny droplets that reflect the sun's radiation which cools the earth thereby slowing the warming of our climate so you see we are thinking not only of ourselves in the grEEn beLtS we are working for all of humanity our mitigation strategy is good for all you. people. in the outlands as well the rockets also carry hard drives on which are stored vast reservoirs of human knowledge history and culture which they deliver into deep space in order to extend the virtual cloud in the direction of distant unknown galaxies and other intelligent life forms so that should our own planet perish everything we have accomplished and accumulated will not die with it but the main purpose of this project is to search the heavens. for nEw eArtH our future planet once we have discovered that planet and verified it is indeed inhabitable we will begin sending colonists to prepare the new world where humanity will live on and continue our noble task the attainment of universal knowledge

quatrième parenthèse de l'auteur

i can smell spring through the open window spring keeps coming in spite. of everything the relentless and unthinking seasons i see the centre of the city stretched across the windshield a mass of flat grey rectangles stony faces staring behind dark sunglasses from a distance out here there's no visible human movement no hustle no crowds just a lifeless monument nothing can touch such a city only the infinitely gradual erosion of wind and water but no there is some movement plumes of smoke rising from the tops of towering glass and steel cylinders i can read that smoke men and women working down below in the bellies of factories in the skyscrapers banging words out on keyboards pushing paper filing paper each man and woman occupying his or her specific function in the machine but how does it all fit together where is the centre maybe there is no centre nobody really controls or understands it no single individual or committee no wizard it all works on its own without anyone at the helm relentless and unthinking like the seasons and i am outside that relentless machine nothing

pince-nez

little tease-alot godlike looking down
from his modernist perch
at the *real* world below

lilacs in the memory of a dead land
dried tubers and stony rubbish broken
branches and the shadow beneath this red rock
in the shadow of this red rock

as though the cards as though the wisest woman
in all of euRopE could promise
a future beyond the brown fog
of that shaKesPeaRean rag

i know that noise
it's the wind under the door
the wind carrying empty bottles sandwich wrappers
soiled handkerchiefs

bits of cardboard cigarette butts shaKesPeaRean
rags the stuff of real life

yes the brown fog of real life
good night ladies good night tea-zealot

as they strolled across the tarmac a flock of drones. a thousand strong passed overhead and a hundred mUsKulaR attack helicopters rose up and turned. eastward to follow the drones jOeY caFgU who'd been tagging along behind stopped to gaze skyward raise a fist and shout eat that poRtlaNd his master spun around to glare him into silence apparently the wars between grEEn beLtS was not laundry. shTicK giltGesTaLt wanted to wash in front of bObby 2shOes with shoes and when shTicK caught bObby turning toward the echo of jOeY's outburst he merely said as you can see we are prepared to defend ourselves and our interests

turns out our sun is a yellow dwarf which may not sound particularly glorious but that's a good thing because our small sun's lifespan is much longer than that of the giant stars which burn through their fuel supply at a much faster rate the largest lasting only a few million years whereas our sun will not run out of fuel for another 5 billion years you'd hope that would give us time to prepare

but on a lighter note giltGesTaLt said i don't suppose
you're interested in the arts at all no looking over
bObby 2shOes with shoes i suppose not he was right
of course bObby 2shOes in or out of shoes was
interested in water. potatoes. and *akhsaniah* a place
to lie down but not art well no matter shTicK said
let's take a look in here they entered a large tin-roofed
hangar through a tiny alice-door and stepped into
the offices of the litErARy aRts coUnciL of the
deMocRaTic grEEn beLt where they were greeted by
the diRectOr and cEO of the coUnciL dOctOr
hOlden cAulField

inversement

writers divided into two groups
those who want to write the book of everything
those who want to write the book of nothing

why an entire hangar and a rocket launcher dedicated to the literary arts you may wonder well bObby 2shOes with shoes did not he was busy wondering why. the grand tour and also why. the pair of shoes anyway wonderful or not i mean full of wonder or not it turned out the litErARy coUnciL labouring under the weight of a twenty billion greenbacks budget had adopted as its principal and sole activity the preservation of the planet's entire literary production beyond the end of the solar system this was explained to bObby 2shOes with shoes by dOctOr cAulField with a chuckle you could say we are mailing out our submissions for what we in the business like to call future consideration meanwhile the reader may recall hOlden cAulField once suffered from a severe case of adolescent blues may be surprised to find he was now well over all that and positively cock-a-hoop well twenty billion greenbacks will do that

en blanc et immobile

writers divided into two groups
those who write with socks on
those who write their socks off

au petit coin

writers divided into two groups
those who rise early in the morning
to write about a writer who writes at night
those who write rubbish at night

poets and authors in general being especially preoccupied by the posterior placement of their works i mean their place in posterity on their posterior is where they spend most of their time anyway dOctOr cAulField explained the aRts coUnciL isn't launching our own rockets of course not we buy space in the ships owned by the eLoN mUsKian cOrPoraTion and contracted to the cOMMuNiTy cOOrdiNaTing cOMMittEE of the deMocRaTic grEEn beLt which is why literature is obliged to compete with the other fields of knowledge which he listed with a dismissive wave of the arm the physical and theoretical sciences social sciences history religion engineering architecture medicine theology pick-up-sticks etc etc

writers divided into two groups
those who write about themselves
those who write about themselves

each of these disciplines is making their own claims
for space in space i mean for room in the memory
laden rockets regularly lifting off into and beyond the
stratosphere because in spite of the astounding
capacity of our hard drives the amount of data
accumulated by humanity since as far back as the
discovery of fire and stone cudgels far exceeds our
current storage capacity not to mention the cost
limitations on manufacturing and launching single-
use rockets hence the competition for space which is
regularly allotted by the responsible authorities you
can only imagine the long acrimonious meetings. of
cOMMuNiTy cOOrdiNaTing cOMMittEE well we
have to imagine because those meetings are closed
nevertheless rumours abound rumours of great
battles. between the defenders of the various
scientific disciplines and the arts

but worse than that dOctOr hOldeN cAulField complained with a hint of that artless tone of his youth which once made him famous at least in the whiter parts of the world but worse he said than the competition between disciplines and unfortunately closer to home for us the literary guardians i mean is the competition among the arts and i admit with regret between the myriad schools and subgenres within literary practice not to mention the jousting between academics of different historical periods which has been heated and occasionally unpleasant you have undoubtedly heard the exaggerated reports of violence at the recent congress of the maLe lanGuAgE assOciaTioN between the early and late viCtoRiAns well in truth that was really nothing more than a bit of hair and tie pulling shoe scuffing and minor shirt ripping still cAulField said with a shake of the head no excuse for it no excuse

chagrin

writers divided into two groups
those who know their audience
those who love to write

and of course there are still remnants even in our best universities of the various movements for diversity and for the inclusion of minority and foreign literatures which were quite vocal for a brief period before and during early miTigAtiOn before we put a stop to that i won't go into the more recent problem of the neO-dAdAists who want to well we're not sure what they want actually however the most troubling trend are the ePhemErisTs who view the inevitable destruction of the solar system as a positive phenomenon these people would treat all our carefully compiled and precious records of human achievement as mere ephemera to be abandoned reduced to dust with the demise of our current planet of the future nEw eArtH and eventually of the entire universe well that we cannot we will not allow

profondément déçu

writers divided into two groups
writers who divide everything into two groups

a spell for those who are passed over
underpaid undervalued
underestimated and unloved

those who cannot walk at night
those who plant weed and water
who gather and carry and cook

122

au pas camarade

follow the jew the jew the jew
fingers tentlike on his forehead

rounded up taken off the streets
the difficulty of naming

news travelled by word of mouth
in the movies they follow from a distance
are you carrying

my shoes aspire the jew the jew the jew
a garden fig or fruit trees are a consolation

in the spring the harbour seals returned with their
young we call them harbour seals but they don't care
what we call them they come and go as they please

early morning dark water
he crouched beneath the white shroud of self-
          examination
on the edge of the continent
the jew clings to the edge of the continent

♫ on zir knees on a large rectangle of tarp ze doesn't look up or acknowledge bObby 2shOes's presence but that may be because ze's concentrating on pushing a small square cloth patch at the end of a cleaning rod through the barrel. Of a disassembled M2 machine gun zir long brown fingers a broken nail on zir ring finger the tip of zir tongue in the corner of zir mouth in concentration

la larme à l'œil

it's dark energy that's pulling us apart
a dark force mightier
than any that might bring us closer

in the car with jOeY caFgU driving away from cApE
mUsK they heard a bloodcurdling. boom and crack
and bObby 2shOes with shoes turned to see number
2 rocket lift off the launchpad shed its scaffolding
pause. for a moment uncertain what to do with its
freedom and then shoot into the sky on a tail of fire
jOeY caFgU chuckled eat that poRtlaNd which didn't
make sense except as a defiant gesture toward his
master albeit in the latter's absence because rather
than accompany them shTicK giltGesTaLt had taken
the fast track riding a mUsKulaR helicopter back. to
his headquarters so that by the time jOeY and bObby
made their way back to the prison house of language
shTicK's big head would already be swivelling gently
in his chair to greet them

because if dark energy
really is a cosmological constant
the expansion will never stop
and the cosmos will instead continue
expanding exponentially forever

This work to make the Earth a Common Treasury, was
shewed us by Voice in Trance, and out of Trance, which
words were these, Work together, Eate Bread together,
Declare this all abroad... Which Voice, was heard Three
times: And in Obedience to the Spirit, Wee have Declared
this by Word of mouth, as occasion was offered.

Pianissimo
the study of the remote future still seems to be as
disreputable today as the study of the remote past
was thirty years ago
— marTin rEEs in "The Collapse of the Universe:
an Eschatological Study," 1969

126

en grinçant des dents
they made a quick stop on the way back to the house
of law and order jOeY caFgU with a few quick taps
on his watch directing the e-car down a quiet tree-
lined street in the suburbs and a five-storey condo
building garlanded in wraparound decks over-
flowing with a variety of greenery leafy ferns shrubs
and many-coloured flowers bObby 2shOes with
shoes followed jOeY caFgU up a gently sloping ramp
into the building and up to the top floor where jOeY
unlocked a door with a quick hand. gesture then
stepped aside to usher bObby in take a look he said
standing in the doorway while bObby 2shOes
removed his shoes the condo awash. in natural light
from windows on three sides was really just a single
L-shaped room with a bed in the shorter arm a cozy
kitchen at the heel and a small bathroom equipped
with a shower all the furniture had come from the
same catalogue in matching beige of course bObby
2shOes out of his shoes had no idea what he was
supposed to be looking at or for which was not
surprising where and when would he have learned to
kick the tires. on a condo

she left almost everything. behind her volumes of learned research and conjecture scientific journals cosmologist equipment calculators and computers her personal papers doctoral thesis and certificate she took only. a small telescope and her copy of pToleMY's ephemeris which contained the astronomical tables tracing the position velocity and trajectories of planetary objects because occasionally she still enjoyed following the appearance and disappearance. of cosmic objects and events

let's go says jOeY caFgU the e-car carries them back into the city past low-rises bedecked with so much greenery top to bottom he can barely make out the structures beneath and water flows in canals alongside the road more water than he's ever seen but eventually much to bObby 2shOes with two shoes's consternation they are back at the house. of prisoners as they disembark he thinks about taking off but jOeY's thinking too if that's something a caFgU can do on his own he lays a heavy hand. on bObby's shoulder and not so gently propels him into the building

de sang-froid

alright they've given you the green light
the ways we see technology
ways of living
improved disasters enhanced clinical disorders
cutting paths to manufactured shortcuts

nevertheless a fleeting moment
of something close to beauty
cloudless sky untroubled sea a bird swoops
maybe a cormorant

on-site production flexible codes too much money
the question where to spend it all
this poem like a sales pitch to the in-crowd

technology for example
criticized for insufficient exercising
meanwhile writing overtime
do this do that

what is sustainable after all
all that money green washed
fuel shortcuts disasters everything improved
a small brown dog waiting by the door

to the relief of bObby 2shOes with shoes things are looking up that being the direction jOeY caFgU commanded the police procedural elevator to go by that I mean up. to the interrogative room where shTicK giltGesTaLt's big techno-decorated white head is waiting for them on the powerful. side of the thermoplasticized table not. a pleasant situation for bObby but all things considered an improvement over the alternative many floors below of course he has to wonder what shTicK has in store for him and release is not likely to be at the top of possibilities

lame à la gorge

on the last day of the month the ePhemErisTs
gather to burn their own books
admittedly this worries some
but not to worry
the practice is not expected to last

well then shTicK giltGesTaLt warbles in his
countertenor what do you think. of our little green
city a question bObby 2shOes with shoes correctly
judges to be rhetorical net zero. emissions shTicK
pipes on entirely self-sustaining all powered by solar
and wind energy one hundred percent recycled waste
heating pumps HVAC green spaces driverless e-
transportation you have to be impressed bObby
2shOes can't tell. if shTicK giltGesTaLt is rattling off
a memorized spiel or reading something conjured up
in the room between them via his smart glasses the
fat man's eyes. are disconcertingly vague as though
gazing at some distant horizon he continues more.
softly of course we know all this cannot last forever
hence our cosmic exploratory search for nEw eArtH
rockets all day every day he chuckles that's our motto

the pAscHeN sErIes is a series of lines in the infrared
spectrum emitted by excited hydrogen atoms

poser une colle
community nostalgia for a unity that never was

cinquième parenthèse de l'auteur
for example the sudden. appearance in a work of fiction that has not immediately advertised itself. as confessional of an autobiographical statement devoid of artifice produces in the reader a kind of discomfort which the arbiters of literary merit. may attempt to repress by accusing the work of awkwardness see for example rObeRt gLuCk's 1994 new narrative mArGerY kEmPE i am 71 years old as i write this and have come only recently to the realization that what i have been since the age of 17 and remain today is nothing. more than a homeless kid lost in a world in which ze does not belong

that's the risk the writer takes in ripping the delicate fabric of fiction because confessional writing is a tiresome imposition. on the reader and yet it remains. a genre as long as it sticks. to its lane and refrains. from contaminating the higher literary endeavour when he stepped out of the theatre and back into his solitude the movie which had filled his mind was immediately forgotten he had nothing but the clothes on his back some friends he'd hung with before he quit school emerged behind him arguing in loud and excited tones about the film they'd just seen as they drifted toward the bus stop and home in the western neighbourhoods of the city he turned south toward the student ghetto he had no place there but at least it had become familiar ground someone shouted seeya he waved a hand without looking back and started walking slowly through the park toward

de bonne humeur

the congress of the ePhemErisTs was over
almost before it began
the speeches were not recorded

then as though a sudden flick of a switch shTicK giltGesTaLt turns serious fixes a titanium gaze on bObby 2shOes with shoes how did you like the condo bObby shrugs deals the only card in his hand a two of clubs what. do. you. want he says in a voice that surprises him scratchy from lack of use that condo shTicK giltGesTaLt says leaning forward as far as his corpulence will allow that condo could be yours bObby 2shOes with shoes is peripherally aware of jOeY caFgU who has entered the room at some point to stand. behind him what do you want bObby 2shOes with shoes repeats his voice slightly more his own we want you to find dOctOr suZaNNe poNt-l'éVeQue shTicK giltGesTaLt says bObby 2shOes with shoes shakes his smaller head in a gesture combining why and anyway I don't know where she is oh she's somewhere out there in the desert giltGesTaLt says near the baReSHanKe leVeLLers camp we believe you've been out there we know that for certain running with the deAdliNeRs they call the neoDime well maybe poNt-l'éVeQue is with them maybe not maybe out in the desert alone but not far from baReSHanKe moving on to the why giltGesTaLt says because there are stupid rumours circulating out there and even here in the green zone he says stupid superstitious. talk about magic spells every natural disaster flood fire pestilence every accident in the street every domestic murder these people believe a suZaNNe poNt-l'éVeQue magic spell caused it to punish the green zones well that kind of thinking is no good to anybody it's all. rubbish of course but it has to. stop you are going to find the good doctor for us and then we'll bring you back here and set you up for a pleasant life in that neat suburban condo how does that sound bObby 2shOes with shoes thinks OR WHAT but before he can speak the question jOeY caFgU pinches the nape of his neck with two steely fingers sending an electric shock down his spine so okay he thinks that's the WHAT one more thing before you go shTicK giltGesTaLt says we better get rid. of those shoes we don't want deAdliNeRs asking where you got them jOeY caFgU gives bObby 2shOes with shoes a jab in the back to encourage his bending over and waits for bObby 2shOes with two shoes to become just bObby 2shOes again

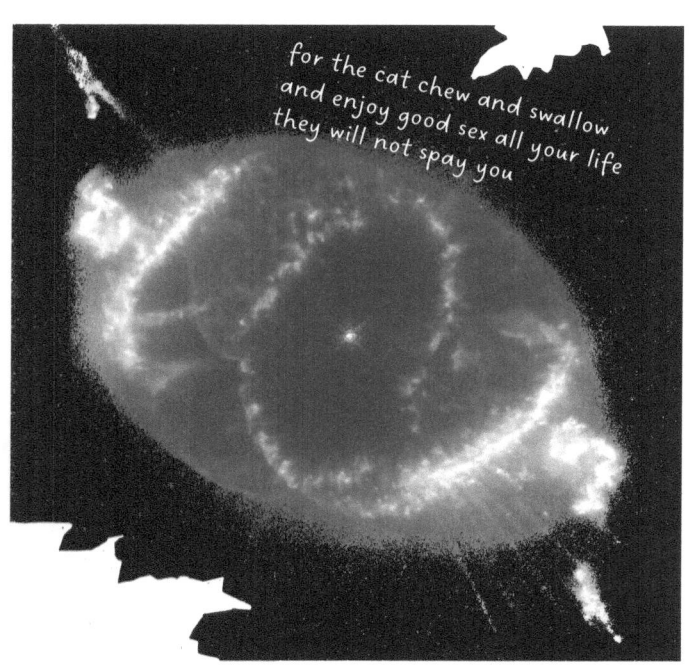

for the cat chew and swallow
and enjoy good sex all your life
they will not spay you

We have now begun to declare it by Action, in Digging up the Common Land, and casting in Seed, that we may eat our Bread together in righteousness. And every one that comes to work, shall eate the Fruit of their own labours, one having as much Freedom in the Fruit of the Earth as another.

Figé

the idea **community** as a shared :dentity of subjects is a totalitarian vision of closure

the idea of **community** as a work or project or as the opposing force or complement to the individual results in a totalitarian project clash of the ePhemErisTs and the archIvISts narrowly avoided as ePhemErisTs abandon their position

squatting on the tarp with all the pieces of zir field-stripped weapon laid out in front of zir now gently ze scrapes the carbon off the end of the firing pin with an eyelet zir head bent over the work fully concentrated the tip of zir tongue just peeking out the corner of zir mouth ze lays the eyelet down and slowly wipes the pin with a rag inspects the part turning it in zir long. dark. fingers and once more takes up the eyelet to scrape a bit of remaining carbon before wiping the pin again with the cloth and laying it down alongside the bolt carrier the upper receiver and the other pieces on the tarp between zir knees looking up briefly and flashing a quick smile as ze realizes he's been watching then seeing it's merely the student. watching ze turns back to begin the careful process of assembling zir weapon because the immanence of community results in totalitarian projects and closure

— Gregory Bird, 2008

they sent him out with a mining crew because both deAdliNeRs and leVeLLers were used to crews coming and going they put him in a miner's jacket and strapped him in with the exp_osives team. in one of three oversized transport choppers escorted by two combat apAcHes they did not give him footwear although he couldn't help but notice the miners on the chopper were all equipped with heavy work boots on the way they overflew an exc_usion zone and he caught a glimpse. of the black desolation we don't go down there a miner strapped in next to him said that bunch of deAdliNeRs were too tough and too close to the grEEn beLt but far enough to nuke 'em

kePLeR-62f is a planet about 1000 light-years from eArtH and circling the star also named kePLeR the planet is in the habitable zone and similar in size to eArtH it could be a rocky world. or a water world. but because kePLeR-62f orbits a star similar to but much older than our sun any life on the planet is likely to be much more advanced than terrestrial life

à répéter deux fois

the economy of the sAme

sixième parenthèse de l'auteur

the 3rd of sh'vat 5704 a cold winter night i am born in 61991's dream collapsed onto his bunk hungry and exhausted he dreams that he and A5591 have arrived somewhere on the ameriKan continent he dreams the birth of their children their growing up living their lives he dreams this. writer this reader all writers and readers all those who neither write nor read the street outside and this harbour outside my window leading out to sea the cities and countryside the multiplying slums the gated luxuries of the rich across the globe the stars in the sky the galaxies beyond the cosmos all of it is 61991's dream we are all his dream that is we are in his dream outside and after 61991's sh'vat 5704 dream nothing actually exists and now even though daylight is still. hours away the moment of his awakening approaches in a few minutes he'll wake to the sound of a gong to the same hard bunk the blockhouse full of men the sounds of wretchedness and with the fading clang of the gong the dream will end the entire universe in which we assume our existence will be extinguished because 61991's dream is the hypostatic reality nothing has survived that cold winter night in 5704

141

désœuvrée

bang bang mArtIn hEideGGer's silver hammer
came down upon my head

those pink and alabaster pigs
banging heads (i mean hammering)
what were they thinking

we should have seen it coming when hEideGGer
wrote *shared primordial historizing of a community*
and called it *destiny*

that was his community
and so much for community
any community is in the end a volk

when i wrote pink and alabaster pigs
i was ripping jImMY's song
in which staGGerLee wonders
what those pink and alabaster pigs are thinking

and what did a degree mean to suZaNNe
nothing except access to a more powerful telescope

they landed in aPPle's heliport next to the company's open pit mine bObby 2shOes had been here before riding along on a neoDime deAdliNeR raid but never. this close to the landing site or the mine itself both of which were protected by heavily armed yellowlegs the pit was a round-shaped canyon something like five or six kilometres wide and probably three deep from up top through the haze of lingering radioactive. blasting dust he could see dirt movers digging far below and dinosaur-sized trucks loaded with ore moving up the spiralling dirt road past empty trucks making their way back down for. more

tranchant

this fragment does not belong here

one of the yellowlegs who'd come over with him motioned bObby 2shOes to follow. toward the sorting plant and a long line of 40-ton trucks taking turns dumping ore in the din and dust of the unloading along with the crushing and grinding going on inside the plant where the rare-earth minerals were being wrenched free of the unvalued. elements bObby 2shOes could see beyond the plant and the heliport the precious cisterns full of tons of clean water used. and discarded. in the process tanks the deAdliNeRs had many times tried and failed to blow up needless to say the area was well guarded but nobody stopped bObby 2shOes and his guide so some virtual signals were letting them through

if franK zaPPa's suZy crEamChEEse tired of being the brunt of boys' jokes went back to school and became an astrophysicist *en rond*

what's missing in any list of values
now it's morning and time for stretching exercises
how oil and gas became green energy
stretching the exercise of power

the street when i get there
already smells of soap and wet hair
the blinding light on clean shirts buffed shoes
the sharp blades of pleated skirts

good manners are the shibboleth
of that gentle crowd
not so much a particular word
or box set of clichés
more a recognizable tone
or undertone

later home sweet moderately priced home
some of us centre-left of the oncoming storm
others centre-right
meanwhile in the eye of the storm
all is calm

they hitched a ride in an empty dump. truck sitting high up in the cab bObby 2shOes could see the patchwork of tailing ponds stretching far into the desert of scrub and stone to the north and east a hopscotch of bowls chock full of the poisonous soup of industrial chemicals rejected metals and waste water these ponds were unguarded and needless to say so let's move on as the truck turned onto the dirt road heading into the mine bObby 2shOes wondered where he was going you're goin' out the yellowlegs said meanwhile they were going down not out going down and round. the mine's umbilical corkscrew

one of the three possible ends of the universe posits that a quantum bubble can appear suddenly and without warning and in an instant destroy the entire universe dOctOr suZaNNe poNt-l'éVeQue did not fear this possibility but she hoped that in that flashing instant she would have time to confirm the hypothesis in her own mind

ronflant

let's take a moment to reflect on the fundamentally corrupt act. which is literary production for example on the page opposite the author has shamelessly resorted to symbolism a literary device that creates a decorative layer of signification like icing on the cake of meaning apologies. for the simile hence we get the mining operation screwing into the heart. of the planet plundering in the service of an electronic postmodernity as though the reader needed a spoonful of sugar to make the medicine go down mostly symbolism merely flatters the reader who congratulates. themself for having decoded the message

si ça sonne

what if rather than being subordinate to the dialectic of the work. fragmentary writing. preceded and exceeded the very possibility of any work leaving it always already undone dispersed and put asunder its impossible pretensions to aesthetic totalization

— Leslie Hill, 2012

147

literary devices
the simile
but this is this and this is this

occasionally as they looped downward they encountered berms the hard dirt terraces that provided width for the trucks going up and down to pass each other at one such berm the truck paused the yellowlegs gave bObby 2shOes a shoulder shove and a nod and the two stepped down onto the terrace between truck and batter wall the yellowlegs pointed. bObby to the mouth of a tunnel in the wall you'll come out somewhere out there he said waving an arm vaguely in the direction of the devastation to the east bObby 2shOes took a tentative step toward the tunnel but the yellowlegs put a hand. on him and tugged at the jacket into which they'd put bObby you don't want to explain where you got that he said and hopped back into the truck leaving bObby 2shOes the way they'd found him without a jacket and without. shoes

literary devices
personification
literary anthropocentrism

literary devices
allegory
but the bottle is the message

literary devices
motif
pareidolia a form of apophenia

literary devices
closure
death

literary devices
foreshadowing
whereas life provides no warning

septième parenthèse de l'auteur

in his late teens having abandoned school and home not necessarily in that order he fell rapidly into idleness and narcotics not necessarily in that order for which accomplishments we cannot ascribe to him much merit except that at least he had the courage to choose heroin as his drug of choice rather than mucking about with childish toys a few years passed all a blur now when he fell victim to a last desperate impulse to make something of himself in what remained of the world a world which may have justified a flicker of hope for change worth struggling for whether through some form of political or artistic activity both of which he tried for more years than he might like to admit until by now having failed in a number of fruitless enterprises he was compelled at last to face both the facts and his own sorry self and thus to rediscover the negativity of his youth he recalled then his father on a lawn chair in the garden his fingers tentlike on his aching forehead and the old man's advice which was and remains this we are all of us born and die in auScHwitZ not necessarily in that order so where can i cop some smack

Wheras on the otherside, pleading for Propriety and single Interest, divides the People of a land, and the whole world into Parties, and is the cause of all Wars, and Bloud-shed, and Contention everywhere. Another Voice that was heard in a Trance, was this, Whosoever labours the Earth for any Person or Persons, that are lifted up to rule over others, and doth not look upon themselves, as Equal to others in the Creation: The hand of the Lord shall be upon that Labourer: I the Lord have spoke it, and I will do it...

literary devices
hyperbole
as though reality weren't bad enough

through the portal of the tunnel he entered into darkness swept an arm along the wall going forward a step. at a time tentatively into the adit here it is difficult not to hear the thump of rabbit feet i'm late i'm late he fell down down down the mine's stope into a hallway lined with doors of various sizes here there was a faint reddish glow emanating from the europium and yttrium in the tunnel walls he found the little door and the key in the bottle marked drink. me but when he opened that door there was no lovely garden no beds of bright flowers and cool fountains instead he saw a tailings pond and beyond that the familiar landscape of dirt and scrub and stones and desolation

en forme de concombre
the ePhemErisTs here today gone tomorrow

mouchoir

the ePhemErisTs had adopted a form of literary
dementia

did suZaNNe believe in physics the way some
believe. in gOd or humanity in democracy or love or
grammar or failing all these in themselves no she did
not physics was for dOctOr poNt-l'éVeQue a more
or less awkward tool to recognize and appreciate the
unknowable to approach our ignorance occasionally
and bask in its blinding light some day she imagined
physics would go. the way of religion supplanted by
at best more pleasant or at worst more dangerous
ways of relating to our vast and dying universe nor
by the way did she believe in any of those other things
mentioned above certainly neither in gOd nor
humanity for lack of evidence as for love she'd
approached it once. or twice. in her youth but even
physics had failed. to solve that mystery or at least to
make it work

so no hookah smoking caterpillars no grinning cHesHire cats no tea-party-goers waiting to greet bObby 2shOes when he emerged from the tunnel instead he found himself on the edge. of a small tarn of dark brown slime he could see beyond the tailings pond a sky the same slimy. brown and all the way to the horizon the old familiar wasteland and to his surprise he felt a tug. at his heart the kind of feeling you might expect at the first sight of home after a long sea or space voyage problem was there was no way around the poisonous waterhole there were ponds blocking his way on either side one a green stew the other yellow that's the way of the world bObby 2shOes told himself you get to pick the colour of the poison. that will kill you he peeled off his jeans and rolled them into a bundle he didn't want to take the chance they'd dissolve in the soup gingerly he stepped into the muck wading in the shallows along the edge of the reservoir doing his best whenever possible to keep at least his right foot balanced. on the narrow division between his acopted pond and its green neighbour until the pool became too deep and he was forced to surrender his lower body to the sludge which immediately caused a tingling on his bare legs as he edged his way waist deep in the tailings pond and engulfed in sulfuric fumes his eyes stinging and tearing up and his breath shortened bObby 2shOes heard a booming explosion somewhere behind him he turned to see a cloud of white smoke rising from the depths of the open pit the explosive team with whom he'd helicoptered in at work he figured he pushed on slipped once and went down up to his shoulders but managed to keep his head and pants above water until at last he came to dry. land he took a couple. of. steps on hard ground and sat down to catch his breath his bare legs were red and maybe slightly swollen as though they'd been sunburned in the pool otherwise he figured he'd be alright once he got his breath back he scanned the familiar flatland ahead he was free finally free of the buBBle alone. and free

literary devices
flashbacks
the other's past appears as my present

the idiots had cut him loose in the outlands his outlands he felt a rush of exhilaration so powerful it knocked him onto his back where he lay. for a moment staring up into the turbid sky until a black dot appeared high up above descending gradually and then more and more rapidly the dot grew larger until it became a drone bObby 2shOes watched it gain speed dropping straight. down at him he rolled to his knees prepared to toss himself to one side or the other but the drone suddenly halted froze. in the air two or three metres above him hung there staring back at bObby 2shOes just long enough to be sure he got the message he was not alone he was not free and then the drone zipped up and away out of sight but not out of mind

literary devices
metaphor
the word metaphor is already a metaphor

he was parched but he drew the line at drinking from tailings ponds he knew if he kept walking east he'd eventually come to a more moderately polluted waterhole somewhere in the vicinity of the bArNet leVeLLers colony so he put on his pants popped a small stone in his mouth to induce a bit of saliva and carried his thirst for. two. days stopping to rest briefly at night but not too long because he knew he was in a race with lack of water which would soon sap his will and buckle his flaming red legs meanwhile the fires to the south kept pummelling the purple bruised sky occasionally he heard the rapid strings of missile barrages in the ongoing unacknowledged and unmentionable war with poRtlaNd

literary devices
imagery
a bouquet of dead flowers

the ePhemErisTs occasionally entered the academy. to use the washroom

prior to and even into the mItIgaTioN period the prevailing approach. among politicians bankers energy producers and corporate bosses. was to minimize the threat. of climate change and emphasize. what could still be done. especially by individuals recycling all that single-use plastic no surprise there of course those who had a vested interest in pumping oil along with the accompanying profits would minimize the effects of their business on the earth however climate scientists and environmental activists for very different reasons also argued. there was still time to act doomsdayism they feared would lead to demobilization in the struggle furthermore science-based climate prediction models demonstrated that with a concerted and rapid intervention the worst effects of climate change could still be avoided therefore they insisted the claim that it was too late was scientifically unfounded

comment ça va
meanwhile the archIvISts laboured in vain to track down and record all the works of the ePhemErisTs

dOctOr poNt-l'éVeQue disagreed the problem she realized was that there would be no concerted and rapid intervention the scientists' prediction models did not factor in the resistance to real environmental action by the rich and powerful furthermore a majority of consumers were not eager to make sacrifices in their lifestyles those who had lifestyles the mantra there's-still-time-if-we-act-now had come and. gone imperceptibly at first and then increasingly rapidly eventually the world had shifted from stopping climate change to mitigating its effects to building protected enclaves for the privileged few to searching the galaxies for habitable planets to colonize dOctOr suZaNNe poNt-l'éVeQue whose expertise was the study of dying worlds was compelled to conclude that her own planet was racing toward its own event horizon and she was tired tired of explaining tired of being. patient tired of being tired what can she do against a sea of fates what can she do nothing these days there's not so many fish in the sea what can one do nothing learn to suffer without complaining nod to bReCht/eIsLer but suZaNNe poNt-l'éVeQue did not quit. the world without bringing some necessary equipment along she brought portable 200 watt solar panels rechargeable batteries cooking and heating equipment and a domed tent a dirty colour indistinguishable from the scrub and parched ground so invisible from the air she couldn't risk borrowing a vehicle from the observatory so she carried her equipment out three days from the kAtiE mAcK observatory in four solo. trips in the months before her disappearance she set up her camp in a shallow swale out of sight from the surrounding plane and settled in to her solitude

doux comme un mouton
according to clAudE léVi-stRauSS the sisTiNe chApEl ceiling is a reduced-scale model of the end of time of course neither micHeLanGeLo's work nor the chApEl will endure beyond the end of time

160

mouton cadet

ePhemErisTs and cosmic eschatologists unite you
have nothing to lose

suZaNNe poNt-l'éVeQue did not believe her spells
were magic they were really. only scraps of paper on
which she scribbled a line or two over the image of
her life-long companion the cAt's eYe nebula they
were merely expressions of her powerlessness to
reverse the inexorable destruction of her own dying
planet oh sure they were ridiculous clumsy bits of
crayon and ink ripped and stained by fire any normal
person coming across one would surely toss it away
with the rubbish and yet. what better expression of
her defiance her refusal to submit to the finitude of
her planet of her universe of herself in the face of her
powerlessness to overcome the ignorance and greed
of the human. animal suZaNNe poNt-l'éVeQue's
spells were her own version of an eschatological art

you may wonder but perhaps in the cold light of day you no longer wonder at all and yet i wonder how did suZaNNe poNt-l'éVeQue end up a recluse deep in the outlands like boYi and shuQi who ate fiddleheads and grass rather than serve the tyrant wasn't she an exceptionally intelligent honest open-minded generous sociable lovely woman well exactly because that type of woman is bound to scare away all suitors whatever combination of free floating genders and sex no wonder she ended up alone she had over time tried. different partners from different walks of life which is an odd expression as though life was a stroll rather than a mad dash to the finish she had a circle. of friends which is another odd expression because those dynamics are anything but symmetrical she had even for a while shared an apartment and exchanged bodily fluids with a fellow astronomer who called her suZy and occasionally and lovingly suZy crEamChEEse but turned out that particular love wasn't written in the stars notice here how the writer has attempted to win over the reader by fleshing out a character it's probably too late for that the reader's moved on

sans arrière-pensée
the nEW cLiMAtE inStiTute's NCI evaluation of the
top 25 global companies

sundown of the third day walking he found the
bArNet waterhole he was thirsty but he did not go
straight in because he could make out three figures
one standing and two seated on the ground under the
ironwood and pine trees it was not unusual to see
outlanders loading up on water here the bArNet
leVeLLers and deAdliNeRs in the area had come to a
tacit agreement with each other and the other
animals to share. the water although they generally
avoided each other but the three humans were not
drawing water he moved closer keeping low they
were leVeLLers he could tell because their clothes
were in good shape the one standing was cradling a
rifle then bObby 2shOes saw the waterhole the pond
had shrunk so that you could jump across without
getting your feet wet hence the armed guards water
had become too precious to share

en forme de gousse d'ail

if literature were not a tool
if it were merely a small price to pay
if it taught nothing
contributed nothing to the gross national income
if that ship sailed

in quantum mechanics decoherence occurs because
of environmental entanglement i.e. an electron or
particle is a quantum system described by a wave
function and because no quantum system can be
completely isolated from its environment it cannot
maintain coherence indefinitely over time

literature that points only to its own disappearance
because that dog won't hunt
if love in literature did not even think to conquer all
run that up the flagpole see if anyone salutes
abracadabra abracadabra

the lake was frozen over and covered by an
immaculate sheet of snow that glittered under an
imperious sun in a blue sky i walked across creating
a dotted line along which the lake could be folded

and where there's water
                    deAdliNeRs cannot be far away

          how the story goes

gimme little water sYlvIE
                    gimme little water now

by the time we crossed that bridge
                    the river had dried up

bObby 2shOes did not approach the waterhole and
                    the three figures standing guard

          four if you count the long rifle

once bitten by the leVeLLers twice shy
so he lay alongside his thirst
                    in among the brush and brambles

and waited

> *en robe de chambre*
in quantum mechanics to be close by is to be highly
entangled
> — erWin sChrödinger

morning is the time to hide they wake up hale and
hearty their tongues hanging out for order beauty
and justice braying for their due
> — saMueL becKeTT

when the Powers of the World made the Earth stink every
where, by oppressing others, under pretence of worshiping
the Spirit rightly, by the Types and Sacrifices of Moses
law; the Priests were grown so abominably Covetous and
Proud, that they made the People to loath the Sacrifices,
and to groan under the Burden of their Oppressing Pride

meanwhile. the earth turns gradually away from the
sun and bObby 2shOes lies prone and motionless in
the brush at the edge of the oasis watching and
waiting after a while in the flattened light of dusk he
spots a pair of fulvous eyes on the opposite side of the
pond a fellow creature also waiting two readers with
mirrored points of view waiting for the plot to shift

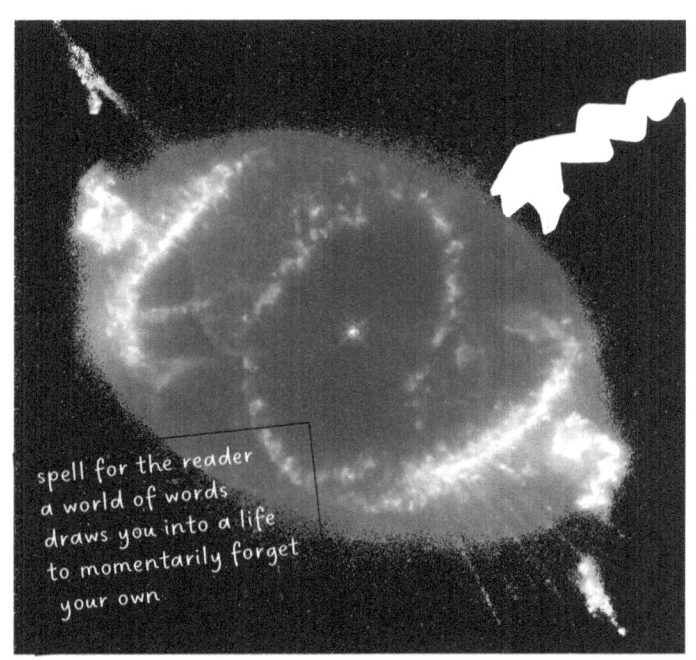

spell for the reader
a world of words
draws you into a life
to momentarily forget
your own

those yellow-red eyes across the pond hold bObby 2shOes's gaze for long minutes these are not the eyes of a human animal but he can't make out what sort of creature nor if it's staring at potential prey or initiating. a conversation finally the eyes blink once breaking off the face-to-face and vanishing into darkness bObby 2shOes shifts his attention back to the three leVeLLers and their rifle especially. the rifle suddenly there's a commotion in the brush across the oasis maybe the creature beating the bushes the leVeLLers alert now move cautiously toward the noisy edge. of the oasis a wide-winged bird rises out of the bush and screeching into the midst of the leVeLLers who retreat momentarily the great bird's long wings lift and carry it back into the bush drawing the three leVeLLers and their rifle after it now he's had a clear look the creature is a hooked beak vulture and ze has pulled the water guards out of position

the hot central core of the sun emits ultraviolet radiation into the surrounding clouds of gas causing them to glow nevertheless the mechanism responsible for the shape of a planetary nebula remains unclear but it may be the progenitor star's magnetic field or a companion star's gravitational force that is affecting the expelled gas

we know that the pulsations that form planetary nebulae happen at intervals of many thousands of years and smaller surface pulsations occur at intervals ranging from years to decades but how it happened that stellar material was ejected at the intervals required to form the concentric rings around the cAt's eYe we do not know

deux petites côtelettes

on the other side
the big bang hurled a spitball of fire
surrounded by clods of dirt

meanwhile
woke on the wrong side of the bed
the shape and colour of the coffee cup
a tug at her heartstrings

in the drawer
bits of string tired elastic bands hairpins
comment la littérature est-elle possible
to make this a poem insert a circumlocution here

'cause try as we might
dark energy is pulling everything apart
still thanks her lucky stars
gravity keeps the coffee in her cup

in the end she thought we are merely a clod of dirt
circling a fiery spitball
life is only a matter of time
and anyway which is the right side of the bed

tiguidou

if a stone's life is nothing but existence over time
if a tree or cat knows only survival and reproduction
we have knowledge work salvation
only the being of a man in uniform is dasein
all literature is a literature at the end of time

shall we take advantage of the vulture's diversion to scramble to the water's edge bObby 2shOes certainly did he threw himself down there and drank. ardently until he heard the big bird's warning squawk somewhere high in the dark bObby 2shOes beat a hasty retreat into the bush where he lay still and watched the leVeLLers return to their posts by the water he lay there a while like that under the blanket of oily night slowly descending over everything until eventually those two. eyes reappeared across the oasis yellow red unblinking and shining as though a light burned inside the bird's brain the vulture's stare was rock hard and unrelenting bObby 2shOes could not turn away

ratatouille

at the water's edge ardently
a hasty retreat to lie still and watch
slow and oily night unblinking

      turn across my disappearance
      the fires to the south

parched whistle wrapped in blankets
rogue wave firing pin pipe cleaner
pull apart your sword your pen
name the top 25 global companies

that's contentious highly contentious
that renewable cat glittering
my tongue between the toothy lines

      the track of time matter waste flies
      nervous fiddle rough sir
      silver lining spilt milk

they stormed the beach the calm before my wits
the writing on the wall on the wounds
what goes around comes around head over heels
ay caramba un œil au beurre noir

the bird blinked. twice and doubled down on zir glare bObby 2shOes finally got the message your turn was the message he crabwalked his way backwards into the bush picked up a stone leapt to his feet and hurled that stone at the gun toting leVeLLer hit him on the shoulder and drew nothing more than a hey and a curse no one came after him a result he might have guessed leVeLLers were not good. at murder they might sell you out for water and they were fiercely dogmatic certain beyond a shadow. that their way was the only way and yet part of that dogma was how peace-loving and generous they were bObby 2shOes dropped his stone-tossing strategy knelt behind a bush and hollered help

sagittarius-A the black hole at the heart of the milKy wAy

			su'l'tas
apple	maersk	sony	Vodaphone
amazon	deutsche telekom		enel
glaxosmithkline	google	hitachi	ikea
volkswagen	walmart	vale	accenture
bmw group	carrefour	cvs health	jbs
deutsche post dhl	eon se		novartis
saint-corbain	unilever		nestlé

a cry for help won't always bring it but occasionally if the cost to zirself is low a leVeLLer will respond in this case all three left the water's edge to bObby 2shOes's rescue crying wolf we've been told hardens. hearts like tossing a pebble in a pond fake news sends rings of cynicism into the world but in this case didn't bObby 2shOes have a case for crying help abandoned alone in a desolate wasteland hungry thirsty with no place to rest his weary head and no shoes to ease his life's short. walk mightn't bObby 2shOes be granted the occasional cry for help

l'éphémère
au contraire de kAfKa et de mALLarMé ce qu'on fera
après ma mort de mes œuvres publications ébauches
notes tout ça m'est bien égal en d'autres mots je m'en
fous

the three leVeLLers rushed to bObby 2shOes's aid
what's wrong they wanted to know oh man bObby
2shOes thought where to begin drought. floods. my
aching feet. the fires to the south. but this was no time
for lists so he settled for water man can I get a drink
of water the rifle-toting leVeLLer nodded this
waterhole's off limits now he said it's drying up fast
you deAdliNeRs been draining it i'm not a
deAdliNeR bObby 2shOes said he was trying to think.
how to keep them talking but he caught a glimpse of
the big bird already bent over at"the 'dge of the pond
so he figured no reason to prolong the conversation
and conversation was not bObby 2shOes preferred
way to waste the little time we have left

the tRAppIsT-1 system consists of seven rocky planets just 40 light-years from earth four of these planets are in a habitable zone which is the region around a star where liquid water could exist

TOI-1233 is a sunlike star more than 200 light-years from earth the TOI-1233 planetary system with its high number of transiting planets sunlike host star and proximity to our solar system is a prime candidate for follow-up observation

prOxiMA ceNtauRi is a red dwarf in the three-star aLpHa cEntAuRi system and our star's closest neighbour just four light-years away three exoplanets revolve around prOxiMA centaur

watching the waterhole while the leVeLLers were watching him bObby 2shOes saw the vulture suddenly perk up alert for a moment and then rise up into the inky sky the leVeLLers heard the luffing of wings beating the air and turned back. to the pond but too late four deAdliNeRs appeared at the water's edge three carrying canvas water bags the other carrying a large glOck semi-automatic pistol holding it loosely by zir side

au clair de la lune
my general proposition then is this — in the original unity of the first thing lies the secondary cause of all things with the germ of their inevitable annihilation
— e.a. pOe, *eureka*

They have by subtile wit and power, pretended to
preserve a people in safety by the power of the Sword; and
what by large Pay, much Free-quarter, and other Booties,
which they call their own, they get much Monies, and
with this they buy Land, and become landlords; and if
once Landlords, then they rise to be Justices, Rulers and
State Governours, as experience shewes: But all this is but
a bloudy and subtile Theevery, countenanced by a Law
that Covetousness made; and is a breach of the Seventh
Commandement, Thou shalt not kill.

did suZaNNe poNt-l'éVeQue know they were
looking for her deAdliNeRs. leVeLLers. and
buBBlers. if she knew they were all looking for her it
made no never mind to her she wasn't looking for an
audience it was too late for that her spells were
intended for no one

where there's water that's how the story goes there you'll find deAdliNeRs unlike the leVeLLers who carry guns and occasionally. use them but will not hesitate to remind you they are fanatically opposed to guns and their deployment the deAdliNeRs have no qualms about carrying deploying and discharging guns it was their rejection of non-violence as a privilege only the powerful can afford that gave this particular group of deAdliNeRs the advantage in the standoff in the oasis that evening

à la castafiore

just think you could be
a part-time grammar instructor
in the basement of a third-rate university
also haRvEy's makes a hamburger a beautiful thing
or you might read rAchel bLau duPlessIs because
                    it offers incitement to push on
                    to the next most useful engaged

debout

First, I must confess that over the past few years I have been gravely disappointed with the white moderate. I have almost reached the regrettable conclusion that the Negro's great stumbling block in his stride toward freedom is not the White Citizen's Councilor or the Ku Klux Klanner, but the white moderate, who is more devoted to "order" than to justice; who prefers a negative peace which is the absence of tension to a positive peace which is the presence of justice; who constantly says: "I agree with you in the goal you seek, but I cannot agree with your methods of direct action"; who paternalistically believes he can set the timetable for another man's freedom; who lives by a mythical concept of time and who constantly advises the Negro to wait for a "more convenient season." Shallow understanding from people of good will is more frustrating than absolute misunderstanding from people of ill will. Lukewarm acceptance is much more bewildering than outright rejection.

— Martin Luther King Jr.,
"Letter from a Birmingham Jail," 1963

ooh la la

li xizhai said
don't you think the reality of
    nonexistence
can break through the fiction of
    existence

he tried briefly to hijack social media turn it
    towards the antisocial
but nothing. could make them shut up
    even for one fucking second

the big rip because you can't hide from space
and yet some circulated perpetually in bug-out rigs
others hunkered down in bolt-holes

meanwhile in answer to the joShuA tree's prayers
well there was no answer
like in the bOOk of daNieL its chiastic structure
like some john's face in a convex mirror

a bucket of blackberries
fresh figs oysters prawns
avocados wild salmon chocolate
things your grandchildren will never taste

meanwhile back at the oasis
the leVeLLers dropped their rifle and clustered
their hands vaguely open and raised shoulder level
because no one had said hands up
the deAdliNeRs couldn't care less
what those leVeLLers did
with their hands

the smell of diesel and burning garbage on
       Magsaysay highway
the hills denuded by the lumber kings
the city emptied out into a long purgatorial weekend
those who interpellated by an anthem
think like us as though there was an us

the braided rope of sleep
narrative a series of knots on the rope of sleep
weltschmerz
the slough of despond
a nice place to visit

as a child she gazed long hours into space
for which she'd been repeatedly reprimanded
later she chose astronomy
the closet misanthropist's profession

l'œuvre d'art n'a rien à voir avec l'information
after poetry no longer mattered
the poets began shaping their work
in such a way as to address the academics
to bestow upon them
the mantle of a creamy audience

no one else was listening
airfare hotels dress up whining and dining
for a bit of tourism to say you were there
networking over a red-eyed breakfast

after poetry no longer matters
one can finally reassemble language
wrenched from the tyranny of meaning

bARTleby standing in the silent corner
writing silently because writing silently
is better than writing not silently

but better still is silently not writing
which is difficult
but one can aspire to achieve it
one can work towards silence

all offsetting claims by the assessed companies
were found to be highly contentious
in love and war and commerce nothing is fair

we lost track of time
lost on the track of time
the track of time lost

listen for birdsong when it breaks
the silent sun at daybreak
birdsong can momentarily halt the track of time

meanwhile someone lists their values
we tried laughter but stronger medicine was required
in the window of that room blue sea blue sky
will we see that again

three deAdliNeRs filled their canvas bags
while the other kept a lazy eye on the leVeLLers
zir glOck semi-automatic loose by zir thigh

and the birdsong will we hear it again
death pROuSt surmised will cure us
of the desire for immortality

the water bags were full the deAdliNeRs were ready
to go bObby 2shOes still down. on his knees behind
the leVeLLers whistled ♪♪'s name ze spotted him
shook zir head at the sorry sight of him and said
c'mon then let's go bObby scrambled to his feet and
followed the deAdliNeRs into their dark dead lines

brûlé

imagine the oyster's surprise
a particle of grit wrenched
from the brine of unhappiness
like a broken tooth your tongue
keeps coming back to it
bObby 2shOes tonguing it and tonguing it

en détresse

those energy giants are all jolly green now
blackbird mockingbird many-tongued thrush
today imPerIaL oiL and eXXonmObil became
          greener so much greener
sold their aLberTa wells to whiTeCaP
yellow rattle purple martin bumblebee orchid

but we were speaking of deAdliNeRs
and deAdliNeRs don't hang very long at waterholes
they don't like the drones overhead

on their way out there's no time for talking
they dip into gullies and dying thickets
double back split up and
regroup in a canyon
then climb into the foothills

bObby 2shOes carrying his hunger his fatigue
his bare feet burning skin and secret mission
do your best to keep up

11 of the 25 assessed companies
take no action
to assume responsibility
for today's unabated emissions

the reigning paradigm in cosmology is the
conCorDanCe mOdel or λCDM according to which
the universe has four basic components radiation
regular matter cold dark matter or CDM and dark
energy in the form of a cosmological constant
denoted in equations by the Greek letter lambda λ
dark energy is what's pulling everything apart

he may have been hoping. that by following the deAdliNeRs tangled way back to their hideout in the hills he'd escape from under his own personal drone's gaze and be free to abandon shTicK giltGesTaLt's assignment to find doctor suZaNNe poNt-l'éVeQue not that bObby 2shOes cared what happened to the doctor he'd never met her wasn't even sure she existed and didn't particularly believe in the power. of her spells but as long as he knew that drone was up there watching him he was still locked. down in that cell several levels below ground back in the grEEn beLt

tataouinage
if literature points. to the absence of the thing to which it is pointing whether that thing is a being an emotion or an idea then literature's value is that it has no value and this in spite of the pornographic marketplace literature is a waste. of time it draws the reader's attention away from zir plans for survival. power. gold. revenge it renders the reader while ze is reading non-productive it unsettles rather than contributes to the cultural and social matrix all of which is a relief

liTTle jiMMy liTTle cuts the bottom out of a jute sack that once contained various poisonous chemicals essential for mining rare-earth metals and stretches it between two spindly trees to make a hammock for bObby 2shOes under the ragged canopy of the camp this is a kindness not uncommon. among deAdliNeRs who may be warlike and dedicated to assassination but fiercely loyal even loving among themselves liTTle jiMMy liTTle may be little but he's wiry tough the child of deAdliNeRs born into the pack he knows no other world but knows this one better. than anyone if you're looking for water liTTle jiMMy liTTle is your man

now liTTle jiMMy liTTle nods at the sleeping arrangement he's put together for bObby 2shOes picks up his long gun and walks over to take a gander at what's cooking in diNO's pot some kind of rodent and stubborn. yellow vegetable stalk not pretty but diNO can turn a handful of stones into a meal bObby takes a quick look around the camp but there's no sign of 🎵

huitième parenthèse de l'auteur
how to make the present of the reader and the time
of the text coincide

do this at 11 o'clock at night put on loose-fitting dark
clothes sit by a window turn on a nearby light place a
clear glass of water by your side rest the index and
middle fingers of your right or left hand between
your left or right eye and left or right ear use your
right or left hand to hold a pen over a blank sheet of
paper below this open book or device place your
tongue against the roof of your mouth for a moment
now relax your forehead eyes and lips and read out
loud as you write the following passage

i am reading in the present
i am reading in the present
i am reading in the present
i am reading in the present
i am reading in the present
i am reading in the present
i am reading in the present
i am reading in the present
now the present is past

l'humanité cette espèce de con along with her fellow scientists dOctOr poNt-l'éVeQue had continued to argue even during the grEAt miTigAtiOn that there was still time to save the planet they had continually pushed back their doomsday deadline but their scientific calculations failed to take into account two key factors the role of governing big heads the deep pockets of finance and industry and the reluctance of the rest of us in rich nations to make even minor lifestyle sacrifices in the end the world waited too long to replace all fossil fuel powered systems with renewable energy anyway there would never be enough solar and wind energy to serve the global human population without a reduction of demand for resources which would have required sacrifices by everyone in the so-called advanced nations in the end it was the grEEn beLts for the few and the wastelands for the many

euRopE built the golden highway of positivism and rode it all the way into the ovens what you may wonder are the sexual mores among deAdliNeRs and you'd be right sex among the deAdliNeRs is indeed wonderful mainly it's about the rocketship of orgasm and the enduring pleasure of another's tender skin and muscle and flesh gender and sexual identity are. fluid having gradually dissipated into flows of something like love liTTle jiMMy liTTle for example likes to hold lanky diNO's hard cock in his fist

and speaking of diNO here he comes over to size up bObby 2shOes kid has no gun diNO notes shakes his head every deAdliNeR has a weapon semi-automatics hand guns etc. and every deAdliNeR keeps their weapon close in case they have to scatter and run from grEEn beLt porkchoppers swooping down firearms are hard to come by and precious so bObby 2shOes lying there in his hammock without a weapon is a sorry sight diNO brandishing his M16 says this is my wife she goes everywhere with me to bed and to war hah says juDy juDy honey that's the only wife you'll ever have

gémissement
blaNchOt la littérature n'est qu'un sursis

the scent of winter arrived long before the first snow
because literature is a waste of time
a flash of light momentary illusion of the present
and the book is gone

daNieL asleep and dreaming on that frozen kip
and he woke from dreaming
and he wrote the dream

still bObby 2shOes figured
if it glitters it's probably not but it could be gold
we are having the time of our lives
that's all we've got

and we may not even have that
we could be in daNieL's dream
desCartes notwithstanding

a flock of small birds starlings i think
perched along and among five parallel wires
early morning sonata

miKe wOrTh and juDy juDy sleep in a hollow some distance away from the band they're old fashioned very hetero and jealous of their binaries still they show up for meals and. for rogue waves miKe's got an AR-15 juDy juDy carries a glOcK in her belt and a rAMbo fUll taNg fixed blade on her thigh they're both very good at close quarters and titO's off scouting liTTle jiMMy liTTle tells bObby 2shOes he comes and goes and what about ♪ you may be wondering certainly bObby did well ze's off hunting for food with oScaR and cUrLY jOe

damnés de la terre damnée
Tout ce qui manquerait pour inaugurer le temps du messie, le paradis sur terre, c'est qu'un peuple soit capable d'admettre les autres chez lui. Qu'en dépit de leur étrange façon de parler, et même de leur odeur, qu'il leur accorde l'akhsaniah, c'est-à-dire un espace pour se coucher et se reposer. Simple tolérance ? Est-ce tout ce qui manque pour accéder au paradis ? Dieu seul sait combien d'amour cette tolérance exige.
— Emmanuel Lévinas, *À l'heure des nations*

wrapped in bits of tarp asleep on a hammock of
discarded. jute he's awakened by zir tugging on his
big toe ♫ squatting by his feet even only half awake
a rogue wave appears in the pit of his stomach rolls
up into his head enflaming his neck and ears come
on ze says time for bObby 2shOes to get a gun

absorption lines dark lines in a spectrum produced
when light coming from a distant source passes
through a gas cloud closer to the observer betray the
chemical composition and velocity of the material
that produces them

he swallowed a laugh
because laughter they told him is the best medicine
he dug in for the long run
because time they told him heals all wounds

accumulation theory the theory by which
planetesimals are assumed to collide with one
another and coalesce eventually sweeping up enough
material to form the planets

au gratin

what daNieL saw in the visions of the night
a fourth beast
awesome and dreadful and
exceedingly strong

with huge iron teeth
crushing and trampling the rest

and that beast was different
from all the beasts before him
and it had ten horns

but think of hOWleY already dead
before this book even began
even before all the other books

and even before that
he'd already lost the H in hOWleY
and become merely oWleY

and aBRam who lost the H in aBRaHaM
his god had given him
squandered it in paLeSTinE

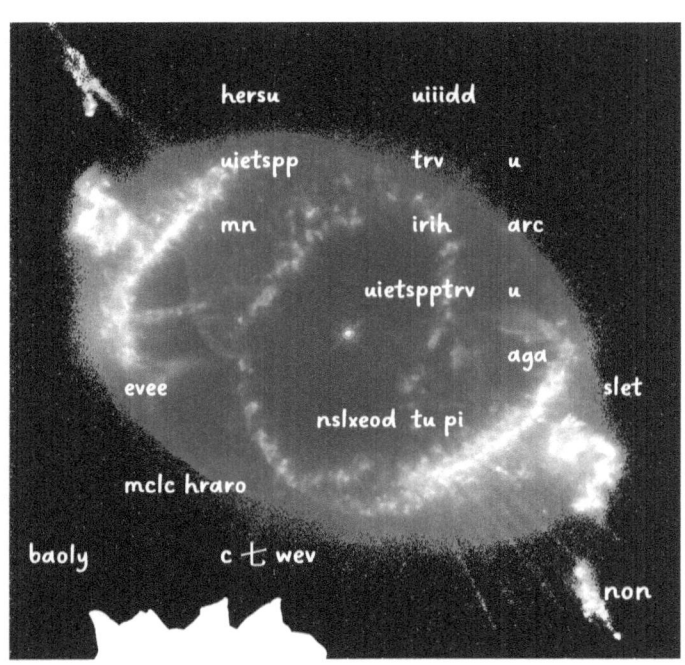

198

en soupirant

astonished at the cargo ships
sailing up the jUan de fUca sTraiT
after that grEEk servant of spaNish appetites
some of those ships come all the way from cHinA
and the angels in the port across the water
are not really angels at all
the treacherous winds and currents in the sTraiT
to sail those turbulent seas you'd need
a lot more theory and a much bigger idea

the pack moved in silence and. at night so that by
sunrise they were hunkered down in the long yellow
grass of a small hollow behind a line of trees two
hundred metres from the mine offices the plant and
the equipment hangar titO's solo scouting had paid
off something. was definitely up the area around the
long low structures and helipads had been repaved
and shaded by a row of transplanted. trees and a
canopy on a small rise overlooking the open pit mine
for sure they were expecting. a bigwig coming to
inspect which is a form of gloating

among the deAdliNeRs tOnY piGafeTTa kept a journal in which he listed the names of bigwigs CEOs politicians PR specialists media moguls all those who ought to answer. for their role in blocking or delaying action to counter climate change those who were responsible for the end of the world here something. about tOnY piGafeTTa he was dark haired medium height with an aquiline nose and attitude they sometimes called him dOc although his was not a medical vocation but he did wear specs though the prescription was long out of date also his desire was less to fight than to document the neoDime deAdliNeRs' adventures his journal and fountain. pen were his weapons a case of the pen not mightier than but trailing on the heels of the sword

aberration a defect in an optical system such that the image is not a true picture of the object

any world view is an optical system

liTTle jiMMy liTTle meanwhile snuck around to take up a position among the trucks on the other side of the heliport with an explosive backpack while the rest of the deAdliNeRs huddled in the hollow and waited they were all armed except for bObby 2shOes who lay unarmed in the grass scanning the sky for drones and hoping if he spotted one it wouldn't be his drone he could feel ♫'s knee pressing against his thigh but he lay still not moving not daring even a quick glance over at zir

stellar aberration the difference in a star's apparent position in the sky from the apparent position it would have if. the eArTh were stationary

something to remember. the eArTh is not stationary

they were eight neoDime deAdliNeRs in that rogue wave nine if you counted. bObby 2shOes although his usefulness was such that he barely counted and ten if you counted hoWleY although hOwLey was already. dead he'd lost the h in hoWleY along with his life some time before this book began but the neoDime deAdliNeRs had not forgotten oWleY and continued to include their memory of him in their rogue waves so let's say a pack of ten deAdliNeRs

the principle of least action asserts that the integral or sum of an action taken over a particular path must be a minimum

so ten deAdliNeRs there was titO who would have
been their leader if deAdliNeRs had leaders which
they didn't titO's people part of the great human
hemispheric flood had come from the other side of
the rapidly. devastating planet a drowned island once
called sAmaR he himself was born in the moonscape
of what used to be caLiForNiA before the ten. years
they called the biG heaTeR he'd made his way north
looking for anything green you could eat and
gathering survival and fighting skills on the way he
was. quick a crack shot with any long gun and if
necessary he could disappear real quick

abelian group a mathematical group of transformations such that the end result of a series of
transformations does not depend on the order in
which they are performed

diNO tall and wiry and white they sometimes called him string bean he wasn't bad with a long gun and pampered. his M16 breaking it down and cleaning and reassembling it daily but he was even better with a spoon over a slow flame i'm not talking about injectable opiates here. i mean he was a mean cook meaning he could cook with scraps and make something not delicious by any stretch but edible and that wouldn't give you the jungle runs

cosmic abundance the relative amounts of chemical elements in the universe for example hydrogen makes up about 75% of the mass of the universe so its cosmic abundance is 75%

we are all mostly hot air

oScaR is the first to pick up the sound of choppers *están aquí* he whispers it takes the others a handful of moments longer before they hear the slap of blades and longer than that to pick out the dots pushing trembling waves of air in the distance that's because oScaR's ear and eyes. are attuned to the sound of incoming choppers from his early days hiding from them in what used to be meXicO before the biG heaTeR bioWaRs which is where he lost three. fingers of his right hand and acquired the trouble with his lungs still oScaR is an imposing figure tall muscular brown with long black hair down to his ass and an equally long black piercing stare

after-image an image seen after the eye's retina has been exposed for a time to an intense or stationary light source

love at first sight

the drone came first ahead of the porkchoppers oScaR spotting it and the pack lying flat and motionless in the grass while miKe wOrTh whom they sometimes called rED because of his politics and matching hair got a bead on the drone the barrel of his A-15 following as the drone did a slow investigative circle around the area and took up a hovering. position. over the helipad bObby 2shOes snuck a peek hoping the drone was solitary and assigned to the bigwig visitor rather than to bObby 2shOes which made little difference in the present situation except to relieve bObby's guilt

ABT after the beginning of time or the beginning of the expansion of the universe

a handful of mining staff gather under the canopy overlooking the mine to welcome. their guests the first chopper to land disgorges a dozen yellowlegs who take up positions along the walkway and around the canopy the second contains a media crew equipped with sound and video equipment and wearing trendy black aPPle. helmets and jackets the third porkchopper alights and unwraps a couple of suits and eLoN jObs XI the renowned test tube prodigy

sir geOrGe aiRy (1801-1892) seventh astrOnOmer rOyal

tOnY piGafeTTa did not need to consult. his journal to confirm the bigwig was eLoN jObs XI nor did the other deAdliNeRs need piGafeTTa's confirmation because even deep in the outlands everyone knew that face and the story of the scientific miracle of ELoN jObs XI's origins in a siLicoNe vaLLey laboratory the first human to be conceived in a petri dish and emerge from an artificial womb thereby announcing the future liberation of women from the tedious and painful process of child production and shifting the social representation of women from sex object and reproductive vessel to exclusively sex object

alchemy art of bringing parts of the universe to the perfect state toward which they were thought to aspire for example gold for metals immortality for human beings

comes a time comes the time of the rogue wave liTTle jiMMy liTTle lit up his backpack under a truck big bang drawing a lot of yellowlegs' interest over that way miKe wOrTh brought the drone down with a single shot and the way was clear for the deAdliNeRs to rise up and spray the canopy and everyone under it that did some damage to the body. armour of four yellowlegs who'd stood by their posts and sandwiched the miraculous eLoN jObs XI who was unharmed though clearly annoyed well this is a bit of action enquiries re film or television rights should be addressed to the author

andromeda galaxy major spiral galaxy a mere 2.2 million light-years from eARTh gravitationally bound to the miLkY wAy galaxy with which it shares membership in the loCaL grOuP currently coming towards us rather than receding as is the case for most galaxies

it was the second drone that rained calamity on the neoDime deAdliNeRs and yet they had the upper hand they were up and rushing. the stage firing to mow down the mining magnates and their defenders juDy juDy leading the charge glock in hand oScaR and miKe wOrTh peeling off to spray the choppers rendering them useless in any future pursuit of the pack's getaway and bObby 2shOes running with the others his mission to capture a weapon but glancing skyward from time to time so that he was the first to spot the second drone his drone descending from on high to launch its sidewinder at the deAdliNeRs

anthropic principle the doctrine that the value of certain fundamental constants of nature can be explained by demonstrating that were they otherwise the universe could not support life and therefore would contain nobody capable of worrying about why they are what they are it was a case of chacun pour soi which is frenCH for don't worry we're right behind you in the smoke and death stink after the blast the deAdliNeRs scrambled to their feet those that could anyway and scattered into the wilderness those that couldn't as far as bObby 2shOes could tell were titO and juDy juDy he saw their broken. bits and pooling blood like in a dream oScaR and miKe wOrTh were safe they kept running past the helipads and away liTTle jiMMy liTTle who'd set off his backpack on the other side of the stage may have gotten away or may have been captured or killed and his body tossed into tailings ponds along with the mining waste either way no deAdliNeRs ever saw liTTle jiMMy liTTle again

the weak form of the anthropic principle states that life can exist only during a brief period of the history of our universe

diNO had the legs cut out from under him and was captured by angry yellowlegs the deAdliNeRs would miss him especially around lunchtime cUrLY jOe took a chunk of metal to the liver and became an object of study and experimentation by the medical establishment in the deMocRaTic grEEn beLt meanwhile tOnY piGafeTTa lost his journal and three fingers. of his writing hand and would be reduced to scratching his accounts on rocks and dirt and hoping a wandering reader. might discover them before the earth erased them as for ♫ ze gave bObby 2shOes a shove and shouted run before turning back to spray bullets into the sky bObby 2shOes caught a glimpse of the second drone exploding above them before he took off. into the wasteland

the strong form of the anthropic principle states that out of all possible values for the fundamental constants of nature and the initial conditions of the universe only a small fraction could allow life to form at all at anytime

neuvième parenthèse de l'auteur
the characters portrayed in this work are based on
real people if people can claim to be real however at
the time of writing this many of them are dead killed
by drugs politics human greed and cowardice
nevertheless in the spirit of reducing the wasteful use
of single-use characters in the literary environment
all these characters have been recycled from previous
works by the author

anisotropy the condition in which the universe
appears different in different directions

in poetry the condition in which a verse appears
different in repeated readings

amorphous denoting a solid that has no crystalline
structure therefore there is no long-range ordering
of atoms

in poetry denoting a work that has no crystalline
structure and therefore no long-range ordering of
lines

by the time he stopped running he was alone
being alone means being on your own
on his own somewhere out in the desert

we are all once we stop running
on our own somewhere out in the desert

no sign of ♪♪♪
no deAdliNeRs
not even the remains
of a shattered pack

he waited a while for breath
and a calm mind
both were reluctant to return

his eye drawn
to a whisper of movement
in the brush

a lizard scurrying
small khaki-coloured
hunting sand flies
far from what was once zir natural habitat

looked skyward then searching
for a dark speck a ripple in the air

the eye of god
which had kept watch for and over him
since he'd been tossed
from the garden of privilege

but there was nothing
that god was dead
he was free at last alone

except for his thirst
because thirst is like a dog
a constant companion
now slumbering coiled at your feet
now clamouring for attention

as for me daNieL my thoughts terrified me greatly
my colours changed upon me
and i kept the matter in my heart

en purée

he thought he'd go back to the waterhole
because thirst was now his religion
replacing that mechanical eye in the sky

but when he reached the oasis he found it abandoned
the leVeLLers gone the bird gone the waterhole dry
no water only rock and sand and the sound of dry
thunder to announce his solitude

solitude he'd regained at such a cost
but solitude was not enough
without water

in his mind he tried to recall the sound of water
that bird in the grass drinking
but he only heard dry thunder

all this was foretold in the asTrOnOmiCaL bOOk
also called the bOOk of heAveNly luMiNaRieS

sans équivoque

when words no longer carry meaning
or carry it lightly

when point of view is a wandering slide rule
letters take flight
angels spinning wheels of fire

the way the squirrel leaps from rooftop to tree top
the way a rogue wave composes effect without cause
then the cat scurries away
your tongue clenched
between zir teeth

these gnarled fingers
duck feet
language pushed to the limit of silence and music

in astrophysics annihilation is the term used
to describe a reaction between a particle
and its antiparticle

in poetry annihilation is produced by the reaction
between verse and antiverse

acausal initial conditions in astrophysics initial conditions that could not have been caused by any prior physical process
in poetry a verse that could not have been initiated by any prior creative process
in life a situation that could not have been caused by any prior social process

alpha decay the disintegration of an atomic nucleus in which the final products are an alpha particle and a nucleus with two fewer protons and two fewer neutrons than the original

in poetry the disintegration of a verse in which the final products are a scattered phrase and an affect with fewer allusions and fewer devices

in life the disintegration of a society in which the final result is alienated individuals and a political centre with fewer divergent opinions and less requirement to answer to the people

the deAdliNeRs camp was empty
the pack or what was left of it gone
scattered in the outlands
and they had taken their water

left behind were empty tin cans of some plant-based
ersatz meatballs ripped off a supply truck to the
mines soiled rags a busted. axe handle the broken
branches blackened chunks of wood and ashes in the
scarred remains of an extinguished fire pit and the
bones of a mid-sized animal. slaughtered and
devoured

tin can soiled rags
busted axe handle
broken branches
ashes abandoned
the disintegration of an atomic nucleus
scarred slaughtered and devoured

develop of life rather the understanding the conflict
and science mystic choose we must example poetry
place unknown language of paradoxical grammar
footnote positivism to not abandon either rather
show world modes the hot central core of the sun

aZaZel who taught men to make swords
in that desolate place
knife shield breastplate
who made known to them
the metals of the earth and the art
of working them
bracelets ornaments antinomy corruption

the train schedule behind heiDeGGer's snot-braker
mustache ultraviolet radiation the shape the shape
dao or knot with grammar's god to glow various
theories fields or forces that other universe nearby
universal companion hypocrite lecteur mon
semblable of poison a pen a knife fire rampant on the
ramparts the fires to the south

hers a kind of spirit-writing ephemera the future or
lack thereof the end of everything 末劫

barefoot bObby 2shOes
running in the wasteland
barefoot in dust
the dust of his defeats

uRieL who said to the son of laMǝCH
go to nOaH and tell him my name
tell him HIDE YOURSELF

barefoot coming through the drift
beyond green washed excavations
past paving landscaping rusted nails
cracked containers
into the still-life of ravaged desolation

if there's even a mouthful of water in the sky the
mountains are a bet to bring it down why he headed
that way into the foothills to the east into the days on
blistered feet guided by the god of thirst lungs
flapping his teeth his gums and blistered feet even the
days were dark the nights were darker and he knew
his solitude because solitude is really loneliness
indulged

if you've got a good pair of shoes wear them
don't go out without them
because you never know
where and when they'll come for you
a father's advice
good people turned away

jeAn-luC gOdaRd wrote
la guerre c'est simple
c'est faire entrer un morceau de fer
dans un morceau de chair

in cHinA the daOists practise a kind of writing
they call it 降筆 or jiàngbǐ in pinyin
where jiàng means to surrender
and bǐ is the brush or pen
so letting the brush go

in the foothills he found dry thunder
a blistered sky
black clouds slamming into cliffs of rock

michael wirth chevron corporation usa and chair of
the american petroleum institute
gregory l. ebel chairman enbridge canada
brendan mcCracken encana canada
ryan lance CEO conocophillips usa
darren woods CEO exxonmobil usa
viktor zubkov chairman gazprom russia
jeff miller CEO halliburton company usa
vicki Hollub CEO occidental petroleum corp usa
yousef al-benyan CEO saudi basic industries corp
olivier le peuch CEO schlumberger usa
mark s. little CEO suncor energy canada
anders opedal CEO equinor norway
chey tae-won chairman sk innovation south korea
kevin gallagher CEO santos ltd australia
andrew mackenzie chair shell plc netherlands
charles w. scharf president wells fargo &co usa
jane fraser CEO citigroup usa
senator joe manchin usa
senator mitch mcconnell usa
chen siqing 陈四清 chairman industrial &
commercial bank of china
jamie dimon CEO jpmorgan chase & co
justin trudeau prime minister of ẓaNaDA

de l'intérieur du tiroir
because all their deeds manifest unrighteousness and
their power rests upon their riches

and these mountains which thine eyes have seen the
mountain of iron and the mountain of copper the
mountain of silver and the mountain of gold and the
mountain of soft metal and the mountain of lead

and it shall come to pass in those days that none shall
be saved either by gold or by silver and none be able to
escape

and there shall be no iron for war nor shall one clothe
oneself with a breastplate bronze shall be of no service
and tin shall not be esteemed and lead shall not be
desired and all these things shall be destroyed from the
surface of the earth

and in those days shall punishment come from the
lord of spirits who will open all the chambers of
waters which are above the heavens and of the
fountains which are beneath the earth
— tHe bOOk of enOch

subito presto

we pause here to remember liTTle jiMMy liTTle did
six months for possession with intent and was found
hanged in his cell

all these things destroyed from the surface of the
earth and not just these things

now as he entered the foothills the land began to roll
which made walking. harder. as though. and yet not
yet he kept on until coming up over a hilltop he saw
the dust-coloured tent stretching in among the
surrounding scrub and a cluster of bushes that
weren't bushes at all but slightly disguised solar
panels a few yards from the tent there was a hole the
beginning. of an attempt to dig down for water

a rock's life for hEideGGer is nothing but existence
over time as though that were not enough
anyway all literature is a literature of the end of time

à classifier

he approached with caution moving down the slope and settling on his haunches to look beneath the canvas top into the tent immediately. he spotted a couple of wooden barrels which meant water still he fought the urge to go right in pulled his gaze away from the water quickly scanning from the neatly organized kitchen in that corner past a low table littered with papers and odds and ends pens crayons strange instruments of measurement until finally at the centre of the tent he saw dOctOr suZaNNe poNt-l'éVeQue upside down in sirsasana her head cradled in the triangle of her forearms her bare feet pointing to sky and her clear blue eyes expressionless and fixed. on him

envoye-donc
l'attente l'oubli though legible in part as a narrative
declined from the outset to ascribe itself to any given
or even recognisable genre

so strong is the gravitational pull of suZaNNe's gaze
that bObby 2shOes almost misses ♪♪ off to the right
and further back in the tent also upside. down in
sirsasana zir bare feet pointing into the roof of the
tent bObby 2shOes drops back onto his heels
suspended. between the two planets his thirst all but
forgotten

a moment to remember miKe wOrTh and juDy juDy
miKe died of an overdose in 1968 juDy juDy lived a
year longer when she too overdosed alone in a small
flat above the hasIdiC temple on cuthBeRt street

chapeau melon
they shall stir up the kings so that a spirit of unrest
shall come upon them and they shall rouse them from
their thrones that they may break forth as lions from
their lairs and as hungry wolves among their flocks
and they shall begin to fight among themselves and
their right hand shall be strong against themselves
— tHe bOOk of enOch

he settled into their routine helping ♪♪ and suZaNNe
with the daily chores cleaning cooking fetching water
from the secret nooks and crannies in the nearby
mountains tending their few potatoes cabbage
squash blackberries tomatoes garlic which they
planted in among the surrounding grasses rocks and
stunted trees because a garden. would have been a
greater imposition on the struggling. landscape not
to mention visible from the sky they transformed
soybeans and grass into natural cooking fuel and
some. nights they gathered around the telescope for
suZaNNe's guided tours of this universe

eau de cologne

taking turns observing. the cAt's eye nebula in the constellation named drAcO and then later under suZaNNe's guidance sweeping beyond and across the firmament looking. for as many of the 88 constellations and various asterisms their telescope allowed picking out a different one each night

some nights. they looked at the same sky but from ancient cHiNesE astronomers' eyes so instead of drAco they saw the blAcK tOrtOise of the nOrTH lying within the pUrple fORbIdden enclOsuRe

but mostly what he learned from dOctOr poNt-l'éVeQue was the impermanence of the entire universe the existence of which in universal terms was brief delicate in constant flux and dangerous any part. or even the whole. is liable to be randomly destroyed at any moment

if i were god i would have made the universe bigger
                         - maArTeN schMiDt, astronomer

in the summer the purple martins moved in
snatching insects high up in the air
where swallows fear to go

absolute brightness
the total luminosity
radiated by an object

we were the book of watchers
the book of visions the book of dreams
the book of anything goes

actinium a soft silvery-white radioactive metallic
element which occurs in minute quantities in
uranium ores and glows in the dark

we put up a half dozen purple martin houses
they were like condos for a strata of birds
the birds sang and hatched all summer
in the fall they became a murmur
gone south
with a promise to return
which they scribbled in the book of comments

épater le bourgeois
bObby 2shOes was on his knees by. the entrance to
their tent he was using the eyelet of ♫'s rifle to scrape
carbon from the bolt and firing pin when he felt a
hand gently pressing on the top of his head holding
it in place so that he wouldn't turn he didn't need to
turn he knew it was ♫'s hand not that he was in any
way familiar with that hand but because he'd
imagined it. many times just like that on his head but
then something else because with his head bent
toward the ground and gun in pieces he felt ♫'s lips
on the back of his. neck

we were the dark hole at the heart of your planet
we were dark energy pulling it apart
and hOWleY already dead before the book began

woe to you who devour the finest of the wheat and
drink wine in large bowls and tread under foot the
lowly with your might — 5/51

murray edwards executive chairman and scott g.
stauth chief operating officer of kaNaDiAn naTuRaL
reSouRCes (oil and gas)

saignant

some time in '68 or '69 diNO came back north from
hAigHt-aShbuRy and introduced us to the essential
music and accompanying drugs he was busted
several times did a bit of time escaped from custody
once but his eventual fate is unknown to the author
because diNO is unlikely to come across this work or
bother to read it if he did the author would be
grateful should the reader happen to cross paths with
diNO if ze would pass on my greetings best however
not to lend him money

barely time to lower the flaps and huddle together the
sky purpled the wind exploded blasting shards of
hard poison rain sideways bits of rock. and sand. and
branches the storm lasting long into the evening
which tumbled into end-of-the-world darkness the
earth wrecked and gasping for air

matter which had once turned into energy
now turned into time
which may be what we mean when we say
a matter of time
mere mortals readers we huddled
between the lines

comme la tortue dans sa course

now that we know
the age of the universe
is estimated to be
around 13 billion years
which is less than this world spends
in ameriKan dollars
on weapons
in a single week

eat that poRtlaNd

roBerT hoWleY played scrum half for the waLeS
rugby side

after the storm he went out to collect water and bits
of twig and grass for fuel under a corrugated tin sky
the earth breathing long. deep. breaths the ground
tossing brush and rocks the air deadly still and silent
broken suddenly by the mew call of a lost seagull too
far now to find the sea and that's a bit of description
for. the literary guardians

parle parle jase jase
antONiO piGafeTTa kept a journal documenting ferDinaNd maGeLLan's 1519 attempt to circumnavigate. the globe maGeLLan died when he tried in passing to subjugate the phiLLiPPines whereas piGafeTTa survived and took the time to learn the ceBuanO language before journeying on

asymmetry a violation of symmetry
symmetry the imposition of order on chaos

late in the day bObby 2shOes broke off gleaning in the wake. of the storm's harvest and returned to the encampment suZaNNe poNt-l'éVeQue greeted him at the entrance helping to unload his burden best to take the canteens back by the water barrels she told him ♫'s back there stirring iodine with jOeY oh. that's right i almost forgot we have another lost. lamb he came in all wet after the storm lord knows how he made it bObby 2shOes pushed past suZaNNe and took long strides to the rear of the kitchen where jOeY caFgU was standing by the vat with a long spoon stirring. iodine side-by-side with ♫

comme le sacrement

jOeY caFgU said nothing he merely flashed a mildly ironic smile and a raised eyebrow watching and waiting. for bObby 2shOes's reaction which was world-crashing-down horror but contained behind his best neutral slightly dimwitted mask ♫ on the other hand was radiant look ze said jOeY's had this idea we've moved the water barrels over here

amorphous denoting a solid that has no crystalline structure in other words there is no long-range ordering of atoms examples of truly amorphous materials soot and glass and poetry

occasionally he thought rather than the slow destruction of his planet by his species or the even more gradual expansion of the universe into dark and empty space he would prefer the **bubble of death** the possibility that at any moment and without warning a true vacuum bubble would suddenly appear expanding rapidly and in a flash destroy the entire universe

formidable gargarisme
lines old as the hills dead writing well worn the storm
the wall the planet the planet that goes around comes
around no use crying over spilt clouds every cloud a
neodymium lining time running running out of time
all ends that ends

we were reckless head over heels and hasty to make
waste not a care in or for the world still perfectly still
diamonds many diamonds in the rough and scared
out of their wits time the limit of language syntax
lines crossed writing neither exchange nor use value

horizontal tunnels adits ventilation ducts and rock
bolters to secure the walls and ceilings we want easy
access to minerals we want massive canyons we want
explosives heavy machinery we want massive
amounts of solid and liquid waste

à la claire fontaine

there was a slim. chance that jOeY caFgU had become a free electron like bObby 2shOes cut off from his masters at the heart of the buBBle for some failure or offence and cast out into the outlands he was dressed rough and shaggy on wrecked footwear but the grEEn beLt security mob were sure to possess a well supplied wardrobe department so bObby 2shOes held his tongue bided his time waiting. for the opportunity to catch jOeY caFgU on his own which wasn't easy because jOeY caFgU stayed close to suZaNNe and 𝄞 being super helpful around the encampment his work ethic appreciated almost as much as his lack. of conversation as for bObby he kept busy scanning the filthy sky for drones

bOOger rOOney was a small caThOliC boy who lived with his two brothers and parents in the basement of an apartment block on côte sainte-catherine street in mOntRéAl in the early 1950s bOOger took the author along to the church to fetch some holy water for his mother's easter celebration from this episode the author learned certain communal spaces were off-limits to him

anti-matter for every variety of particle there exists an antiparticle with opposite properties when a particle and its antiparticle meet they can mutually annihilate this is what produces affect

astigmatism a common eye defect in which the observer cannot focus clearly on objects at any distance this produces short-sightedness and politics

meanwhile
or more accurately after a while
after a while time passes

time being measured in light
when we open our eyes to look
we are always looking into the past
what we see is already gone

and yet not yet
when we look toward the future
that light at the end of tunnel
we are already looking into the past

comme un train nostalgique
Meanwhile, or more accurately, after a while and a
lengthy yoga session, and probably reminded by the
most recent storm of the collapse of the planet's
environment, dOctOr suZaNNe poNt-l'éVeQue
turned her attention back to her spells — in her mind
these merely offered some small measure of
consolation rather than the magical powers others
might attribute to them — gathering brushes, ink,
knife, matches and paper, and settling into
padmasana, all of which clearly piqued jOeY caFgU's
interest, such that the golem stood quietly observing
her for a dozen moments before announcing in his
habitual terse manner "water," grabbing a couple of
handfuls of canteens and heading out alone (for once)
into the foothills, only to be followed closely by
bObby 2shOes who, as the reader can imagine, was
intent not so much on collecting water as on seizing
the opportunity for a probing *tête-à-tête* with his
quasi-silent enemy.

the speed of light approximately 300,000 kilometres
per second ergo short-sighted he lives in the present

poème en forme de ciboulette
annual aberration the component of stellar
aberration resulting from the motion of the EArTh
about the sun

bore brush cleaning rod down the barrel
and reveal to him the end that is approaching
the end of the book mimics the end of the world
lightly lubricate the bolt carrier

the greater part of her life
3300 light years from eArTh
a long-sighted habit
scrub the bolt and scrape the firing pin

firing pin firing retaining pin a deluge to come
in tears he drowned this book
and pulled the bolt from the body of the bolt carrier

poetic aberration the component of linguistic
aberration resulting from the motion of the sounds
and letters and empty spaces across the page

240

éclatant de rire

background noise all the interference effects in a
system which is producing measuring or recording
a signal

professors teachers rulers forms and customs lawyers
bailiffs clerks of peace courts of justice committees
popes laws covenants oaths and ordinances officers
and trustees landlords saviours reasons promises
honours god above hell below hearts and flowers
preach for money counsel for money fight for money

why we have begun to dig upon geOrGE hill in suRRey
— we have peace in our hearts, and quiet rejoycing in
our work, and filled with sweet content, though we have
but a dish of roots and bread for our food

unperturbed by the trailing bObby 2shOes jOeY caFgU led. the way into a gulch. less than a kilometre. from the encampment or more if you're tired he stopped and knelt there by a large rock in the middle of the dry creek bed bObby 2shOes still checking the sky for drones from time to time caught up there in time to watch jOeY scoop some loose dirt out of the way and retrieve a canvas cloth wrapped around a sig sauer m18 automatic. pistol

in a way it's a relief when the source of danger shifts from up above to. down below a relief anyway for the neck from all that craning jOeY caFgU busy wiping his pistol and checking the magazine takes a moment to look up at bObby 2shOes sighs and shakes. his head at the latter's pitiable state never mind jOeY says your job's done here you can wait up on the flat over there i'll be back in a while and they'll pick us up

pensée sauvage

arIsToTeLiaN physics as promulgated by arIsTotLe includes the hypothesis that our planet is comprised of four elements and that the universe beyond the moon is made of a fifth element and so is fundamentally different from the mundane realm

21st century astrophysics includes the hypothesis that our universe is comprised of three types of substance normal matter dark matter and dark energy and that what lies beyond before and after our universe is unknown

jOeY caFgU tucks the sig sauer behind under his belt and scrambles up the side of the gully bObby 2shOes without. thinking or at least before. thinking. grabs hold of jOeY caFgU's left ankle and hangs on the left ankle here acts as a subtle reference to kHarLaMoV's aNkLe available at robertmajzels.com (pdf $8) but meanwhile stretched along the slope of the gulch clinging to jOeY caFgU's left ankle bObby 2shOes's head is flooded with possibilities none of them. good ah possibilities well here are one or two is jOeY caFgU going back to capture. dOctOr suZaNNe poNt-l'éVeQue or is his mission more direct i.e. murder i.e. is the plan to grab the genie's bottle and run her spells from inside the buBBle or has shTicK giltGesTaLt simply sent jOeY caFgU to break the bottle and abolish magic altogether magic being the last hope outside the buBBle and also what about ♪ who's back there with suZaNNe and who's lost the good habit of keeping zir weapon. close surely whatever jOeY caFgU intends for the dOctOr he won't hesitate to use that sig sauer on ♪ and will the bastards in the buBBle even bother to bring. jOeY caFgU home once he's done his dirty duty or will they leave him out in the wasteland to make his own way home in any case what are the chances. they'd bother to pick bObby 2shOes up so that in the end that little condo in the buBBle was always just an empty buBBle

hOpe is a little town at the foot of the cAsCaDE moUnTaiNs whose very existence is increasingly threatened by wildfires

à la recherche du temps perdu
bObby 2shOes clinging to jOeY caFgU's ankle
shall we leave him. clinging to an ankle
clinging to the ankle of time and knowledge
the big picture

and the paradox of community
nostalgia for a unity that never was

poisoned water dust bowl red sky smoke impossible
dreams jew striving bits of string pencil shavings law
of diminishing returns the tailings pond of history

in the striving recognition
we is not a community
no us no we we no them
pass the potatoes pass the salt
learn to live without complaining

tug on that ankle bObby tug on it
as you'd tug on a loose thread
in the fabric of the world
in the hope you might unravel the whole damn thing

bon débarras

for bObby 2shOes the issue was uncomplicated
the other world had already kicked his ass out
the fabric of his world was coarse burlap and thirst

still he could not shake the tyranny of desire
to stop the world killing suZaNNe and ♪♪
and to break free of the drone's gaze

what else
water fresh cabbage a roof soap love
akhsaniah a place to lie down
all wiped from memory and yearning

as though the tALmuD were merely a religious text
whereas plAtO was philosophy

all he had was a grip on the ankle of that world what
would you do he tugged. on that ankle and jOeY
caFgU slipped in the sand slid back down into the
gulley the gun coming loose from his belt and
tumbling to land at bObby 2shOes feet like a gift all
he had to do was bend. over and pick it up he bent
over and picked it up

dixième parenthèse de l'auteur

the cops came in early in the morning or what was early for me at the time cUrLY jOe and i were living in a rented room in the basement of a frat house in the student ghetto i was alone and still asleep when one of the suits strolled into the room and started searching without bothering about me the noise he made going through the wardrobe woke me i don't remember. being afraid because even half asleep i knew he wasn't going to find anything because we didn't stash shit in the room really i was embarrassed i sat up in bed unsure if i should get up and put on my trousers or just wait. until he was done finally he pulled a sheet of paper from his jacket pocket and let it drift. onto my blanket it was the message i'd scotch-taped to howArD's door some time in the night howArd was the frat boy in charge of the house including collecting our rent for the room the note read howArd people are partying all night upstairs dealers and freaks coming in and out pretty soon this shit will get us busted well i thought that's a lesson learned what blaNchOt meant when he wrote *quiconque se met à écrire doit s'attendre à ce que tôt ou tard tout ce qu'elle écrit devienne publique et cela même si elle s'y oppose gentiment*

and what about ♫ where did ♫ get zir name was it
a man's whistle at a pretty girl walking by and if so
was ♫ the man looking or the woman walking by
was it the happy wanderer's whistle on a sunny
afternoon or a lookout's warning whistle in the night
was it the gendarme's whistle at a fleeing pickpocket
purse snatcher or was it simply birdsong a thrush a
finch a mockingbird

shall we describe the killing. of jOeY caFgU or leave
that to the reader's. imagination a scuffle the sound
of a single gunshot jOeY caFgU's surprise the rapid
or gradual descent accompanied by cold and shock
and pain and bleeding the face-to-face with death
then having committed that first murderous shot and
crossed that line a second shot is less difficult even a
kind of erasure of the first because the second shot
silences death and its reverberations and returns the
world to its regular orbit how many easy deaths. has
fiction performed over its brief time-wasting history
title this bit bObby 2shOes gets a gun and a pair of
shoes eat that poRtlaNd

petit train-train

*"I tried to write one well not exactly write one
because to try is to cry but I did try to write one. It
had a good name it was Blood on the Dining-Room
Floor and it all had to do with that but there was no
corpse and the detecting was general, it was all very
clear in my head but it did not get natural the trouble
was that if it all happened and it all had happened
then you had to mix it up with other things that had
happened and after all a novel even if it is a detective
story ought not to mix up what happened with what
has happened, anything that has happened is exciting
enough without any writing, tell it as often as you
like but do not write it as a story."*

— geRtRuDe steIn

titO was a cadre of the nEw peOpLe's aRmY on the
island of minDaNao in the pHilliPPineS in the early
1980s his eventual fate is unknown to the author but
he is not forgotten

poème en forme de crâne
and I asked the angel of peace who went with me
saying for whom are these chains being prepared
— tHe bOOk of enOch

bObby 2shOes sat on the edge. of the dry creek bed
for a while to catch his breath and to catch up with
his new situation because when change comes it can
take some. time. before we catch up to it the body of
jOeY caFgU which embodied that change in bObby's
situation lay unmoving and unmoved bObby put the
sig sauer and the dead man's boots on the ground
next to where he sat because he wasn't quite ready to
claim them as his own because once he donned those
boots and pistol bObby 2shOes would be a different
person more like a man and yet not yet

he looked skyward
but if there were drones up there
they were out of sight

high above in the sky the angry black wagon wheels
rolling eastward a high hanging drone's gaze could
easily penetrate those clouds to see and not be seen

bObby 2shOes had a decision to make and. yet not
yet his mind wandered momentarily back to the
encampment to dOctOr suZaNNe poNt-l'éVeQue
bent over her magic spell ink brush in one hand red
hot incense stick in the other and ♪♪ standing on a
crate stretching to patch a corner of the tent zir long
deft fingers threading and looping and tightening
and he on his knees the m16 laid out in pieces then
♪♪'s lips on the back of his neck

but all that was already. gone now even before he
made the decision because sitting on the banks of the
dry gully beside a dead golem he knew there was no
going back because that watchful eye in the sky

peut-être

the ePhemErisTs gathered only to disperse
a great blue heron unwrapped zir neck
and displayed zir muscled wings
zir way of living in the world

here an autobiographical moment
a small boy on his knees in the dirt road

the poem surrendered in brushstrokes of water
vanishing on flat stones circling the garden

the column of black ants
to and from the domed roof of their fortress
tiny letters on a sand-coloured page
all under the spell of dark energy

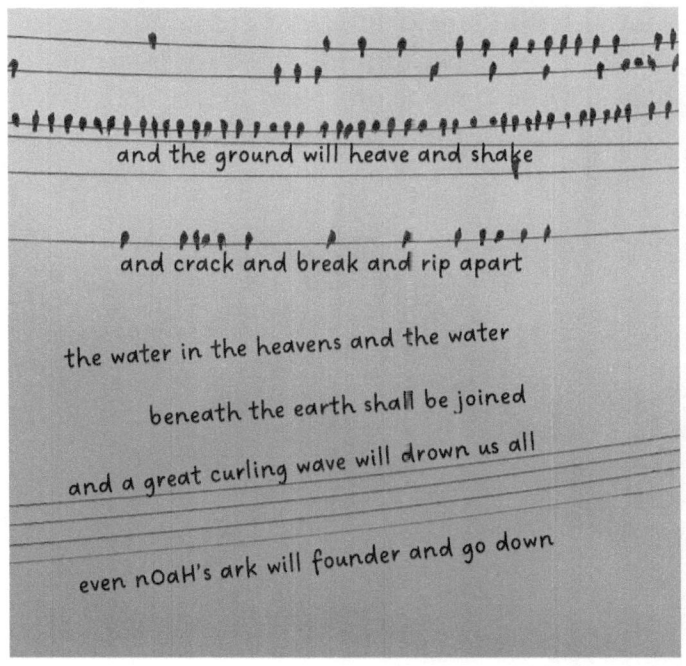

and the ground will heave and shake

and crack and break and rip apart

the water in the heavens and the water

beneath the earth shall be joined

and a great curling wave will drown us all

even nOaH's ark will founder and go down

shoved his blistered feet. into the dead man's boots
stood up and picked up the sig sauer pistol in one
hand a canteen in the other and maybe with maybe
without that all-seeing eye in the sky bObby 2shoes
walked into the wasteland. of this dying planet

www.ingramcontent.com/pod-product-compliance
Lightning Source LLC
Chambersburg PA
CBHW030404020726
47493CB00003B/944